NOTHING CLOSE TO HOME

NISSA HARLOW

NIMBLE HOPE PUBLISHING

ISBN: 978-1-7781397-6-5

Published in Canada by Nimble Hope Publishing
Cover and book design by Nissa Harlow

For all those who feel alone in the world:
Your people are out there.
You just have to find them.

CHAPTER 1

SO HUNGRY

It's hard to think on an empty stomach.

Hunger-induced lack of thinking: That was the reason I found myself standing in front of Joshua and his goons, pretending to be in awe of his mere existence. Really, the whole thing was laughable. There he was, lounging on a homemade throne that seemed to consist of an old recliner and a bunch of dull kitchen knives. What was probably supposed to look like a halo of blades behind his head looked more like a kid's unwanted art project at a garage sale. I wasn't intimidated by that in any way.

The guns his henchmen had stuck in the waistbands of their worn-out jeans? Now, those were a little more worrisome.

"What do you want?" he drawled, his haughty eyebrows raised. I resisted the urge to roll my eyes. Joshua was younger than me . . . but he was obviously ruthless. You didn't end up controlling a territory in the Rift Zone without doing some pretty nasty things.

I ran over a list of responses in my head. *What do you think?* Too snarky. *I don't want anything.* A lie. *The world to go back to the way it was before the Rift.* Impossible, so therefore pointless to mention. I decided to just go with the truth. "Food."

"Yeah? You hungry?"

I bit back another snarky response and merely nodded. Joshua leaned his head back into the circle of knives and looked down his overly long nose at me.

"Think you can handle a job?"

"Depends what it is."

An oily smirk twisted his already-greasy face, causing a red-and-white pimple near the corner of his mouth to shift. He pulled back on the expression quickly. No doubt, that monster zit hurt like a bitch. "You got pinkhands?"

"Would I be stuck in this hellhole if I didn't?" I asked. He wanted a demonstration, but I wasn't in the mood. I kept my fists tightly clenched at my sides. His gaze flicked down, then back up to meet mine.

"Dunno. You could be a spy."

"From where?"

"Outside."

I snorted. "If someone managed to get in, then you've got bigger problems than me."

"Yeah? How so?"

"If someone could get in, that means someone

could get out. Then it's only a matter of time before people start leaving."

"Why would they want to leave?" he asked. But he didn't even give me a chance to respond before leaning forward and resting his elbows on his knees as he fixed me with a dark look. "They haven't wanted to yet. Most kids know a good thing when they see it."

"Sure. Being trapped in a tiny, post-apocalyptic town is every young person's dream."

"Why not? We have everything we need. If we know how to get it." He jerked his chin in my direction. "Show me."

"Show you what?"

"Show me the pink."

"Why? We all have it."

"Do you want this job or not?"

Shaking, I raised my hands, palms up, fingers slightly curled. I tried desperately to still the tremble, but had exactly zero luck with that. Joshua took a deep breath to speak, no doubt to tell me to hurry up and show him, when I felt the liquid energy trickle down my arms, gently tugging on my heart as it went. My hands began to glow, the warm pink aura emanating from my fingertips in wispy tendrils that reached for the sky.

"Is that what you wanted to see?" I asked, trembling with the force of the energy I could feel coursing down my arms. It was getting stronger. Too strong. And if I didn't stop soon, I wouldn't be able to. I yanked my fingers into fists, causing a few pink sparks to squish out as if I'd squeezed a sponge.

"Why'd you stop?"

"Because I'm still learning how to control it."

"It's been three years."

"Yeah, so?"

"I can control it. And I'm younger than you."

"Good for you."

"And I'm a guy," he said, choosing to ignore the tone of my last retort. "It's harder for us."

"Really? I thought women were the emotionally unstable ones."

He shrugged carelessly, caught in his own contradiction. I stuffed my fists (which still felt unusually tingly) into my jacket pockets.

"So . . . can I have the job or not?"

He sucked in a deep breath and sat up a little straighter before sinking back on his mangy throne with a sigh. "I guess you'll do."

"For what?"

"Just a run." He tipped his head eastward. "Other side of town."

"Not your territory."

He let out a sharp laugh. "You think I'm gonna steal from my own?"

"I think you're awfully brazen when it's not your neck on the line."

The words were out before I could stop them. Joshua's eyebrows rose. So did all six eyebrows of his henchmen as they looked at him, probably wondering what his reaction was going to be. I desperately wished I could take back my words and think about my response a little more carefully. Honestly, it was a wonder I hadn't gotten myself killed yet.

"Feisty little bitch, aren't you?"

"Just an observation."

"Why do I need to risk my neck when I've got yours?" He leaned sideways and crooked his finger at one of his goons. The kid was big, already the size of an adult, though he didn't seem to have any facial hair and his face was zittier than the rest of the guys in that room put together. He leaned close to Joshua so he could hear the whisper, then lumbered from the room, disappearing through a door at the back of the space.

Nobody said anything. I figured we were waiting for the big guy to come back. I kept my gaze away from Joshua and his throne as I let it sweep over the rest of the space. There really wasn't much to see, though. What had once been a phone boutique was now just an empty room. Even the shelves that had once lined the walls—where the very first phone I'd ever gotten had been on display—were gone, torn out by looters. I didn't know what they would've been used for, though; you couldn't eat metal, and it didn't burn. The carpet bore signs of trouble, dark stains that made me shudder to think about. But the lights were still on, which was something. The town was a quarantine zone . . . but somebody had obviously drawn a line at letting us freeze every winter, because the power was still on. We had light, heat, and running water. But not much else.

"What the fuck is taking so long?" Joshua shouted, causing me to startle. I whipped my head toward him, only to find a pissed-off expression staring back at me.

"Maybe you need smarter help," I said.

"Maybe you need to keep your nose out of my business, if you know what's good for you."

I bit my lips together to keep from saying anything else. If he decided not to give me a job, I'd have to figure out something else, like crawling back to C-Roy on the other side of town. And I really didn't want to do that. I was already down one baby toe from the last job I'd done for him.

The huge, zitty kid returned, carrying a folded piece of paper. He tried to hand it to Joshua but was waved away.

"Give it to her."

"What is it?" I asked.

"Are you serious? On second thought, maybe you're not up for this."

"I don't even know what 'this' is. How am I supposed to do a job if—"

"Just take the goddamn map and go."

"Map?" I echoed as the huge kid slapped the folded paper into my hand. "A map to what?"

"What does it look like?"

I turned the thing right-side up so I could read the front. It was a simple, old-fashioned map of the town and surrounding area. "I know my way around Kenyonville," I said. "And we can't get past the wall, so the rest of it is—"

"It's marked," he said, interrupting me with a nod of his chin at the map.

"What is?"

"Your target."

"You can't just tell me what it is?" I asked as I began to unfold the paper.

"Stop."

I did, my fingers trembling. "Why?"

"Open it when you get outside."

"Why?"

"'Cause I don't want to hear you bitch about the job."

"Why would I?"

"You look like the bitching type."

And you look like the asshole type, I almost said, but stopped myself just in time.

"Look, do you want the job or not?"

I wasn't so sure. But, before I could answer, my stomach did it for me. Joshua smirked and waved his hand, like he was a king dismissing one of his peasants. Gripping the folded map in one sweaty hand, I kept my gaze on the wannabe king.

"I'll take the job. Just tell me what you want, and I'll get it."

"Yeah, we'll see."

"Yeah, we will. So? What am I stealing from this mystery location?"

"The list is on the map."

"There's a *list*? How big is this job? Am I going to need help?"

"Not unless you're totally incompetent." His gaze raked me from head to toe. "Or soft."

"Do I look soft to you?"

"You wouldn't have lasted this long if you were. Then again," he said, leaning back on his throne so he could do his down-the-nose glare, "you're soft enough to be slowly starving. So . . . we'll see."

I didn't trust myself to say anything else to the little pissant. So I folded the map again until it was a square and slid it into my pocket. Then I turned and headed for the door, careful to dodge the stain on the gritty carpet.

CHAPTER 2

LITTLE THIEVES

desperately wanted to look at the map so I'd know what sort of mess I'd gotten myself into. But Joshua's turf—once a perfectly decent part of town—was a little rough, and the area around his lair wasn't the sort of place you could just sit down and relax in. The streets looked deserted, but I could feel eyes watching. Like, lots of eyes.

People tended to get a bit paranoid after a magical apocalypse.

The afternoon sun warmed the top of my head as I made my way along the street, heading for a nearby park. Despite the evacuation of the majority of the population after the Rift, there were very few places in Kenyonville where a person could get a little privacy. Setting foot in claimed spaces was a recipe for disaster, especially if you were on the turf of some boss who got really pissy about property rights.

So the park was a safe haven, and I was glad to see it wasn't too crowded. Ignoring the harried-looking girl pushing a squealing toddler on one of the swings, I kept my gaze low and headed for the picnic tables at the north side of the grassy expanse. The wooden benches were dry and splintery, covered in unintelligible words written in permanent marker. There were plenty of phone numbers, too, relics from a not-so-distant past. (Not that there were no phones in town. A few landlines still worked. But they were so few and far between that we might as well have been living in the 19th century.) I sat down on the sun-warmed surface and pulled the folded map from my pocket.

The thing was pretty trashed; it looked like it had been used dozens of times already. Messily scrawled along one edge—perhaps as a warning, though it was hard to say for sure—was a variation of the code we all lived by:

1. hand's off pink tickett house's
2. don't mess with you're boss
3. shareing is careing

It wasn't even a full map. It was just a piece of something much larger, torn along the existing fold lines in a ragged square around the town and its immediate surroundings. Various locations were circled, and sometimes there was a list of items next to the circle. Most of these scribblings had been marked with a big X, and it took a moment before I was able to find the only one that wasn't. My heart sank.

"Are you *kidding* me?" I muttered as my gaze skipped over the list. Joshua was one of the younger bosses in town—actually, he was probably the youngest—but that was still no excuse for the stupid crap on the list in front of me: Snacks. Pop. Beer. Weed. Video games. Honestly, it looked more like the wish list of a 12-year-old boy who wanted to show off to his friends.

Given the age of the people who'd been quarantined in Kenyonville, it had taken a while for most of us to smarten up and get our priorities straight. Junk food might've been good for trading, but it wasn't the really valuable stuff. The real treasures were the things that kept us alive: cans of beans, freeze-dried meat, ready-to-eat camping meals. As many of us had found out after the exodus of mature adults, chips and pop were a lousy source of nutrition.

The checkpoints did sometimes give us a few treats, and small amounts of various contraband somehow mysteriously appeared and circulated throughout the town. But if there was a whole stash somewhere, it meant someone had been hoarding. And I was about to walk right into the middle of that and try to steal from some other boss. Niesha, I guessed, as I scrutinized the map. She was bound to be a lot smarter than Joshua. She was also less likely to leave such a valuable stash unguarded. And, based on what I'd heard from whispered rumours in the dark, she wouldn't hesitate to make an example of me if I were caught.

With a sigh, I checked the grody old map one more time before folding it back up. Joshua had given me a dangerous job. He probably didn't even expect me to succeed. If I did, it would just be a bonus. But it wasn't like I could refuse. My jeans were loose around my hips, and I was about ready to eat my own hair if I didn't find something else soon. Using the table for leverage, I hauled myself to my feet. If I did this job, there was no guarantee I would be coming back. So I needed to pick up my stuff.

I hurried down the overgrown streets, taking every shortcut I knew, and the single-story shops and low-rise apartment buildings eventually gave way to more suburban-looking dwellings. Not that a town as small as Kenyonville actually had a suburb of its own. Had it been near a big city, it probably would've *been* the suburb.

The small townhouse where I'd chosen to crash was more of a hostel, really, with kids coming and going. Ayla had been there the longest. She'd apparently gotten there just a few weeks after the evacuation. I'd only arrived in the last few months. It didn't feel anything like home; the people kept changing, even three years after the Rift had ripped its way into the town. On any given day, you never knew who would turn up needing a place to sleep, a place to shower, a place to plug in their useless phone (some kids still clung to them, even though they weren't much good for anything other than playing a few simple games and taking photos they could never share). There was a bit of food, but it was never enough. Ayla obviously had some sort of deal going with Joshua . . . but I suspected she kept the good stuff for herself.

I was so busy thinking about what might happen later that afternoon that I wasn't really paying attention as I pushed aside the curtain of twinkle lights and stepped into what had once been a living room. Blankets, sleeping bags, pillows, and random couch cushions took up the space, and I stepped carefully through the chaos as I made my way to the little nest in the corner. It was a good spot, far enough from any windows that I didn't get a draft, but close enough to the back hallway that I could make an easy escape if I needed to. I had a pillow (some orthopaedic thing made of foam that someone had found on a run but that nobody else had wanted), a fleece blanket that had some sort of faded cartoon character on it (I figured it had probably belonged to a little kid before the Rift), and a small backpack with a few personal possessions. I didn't have a lot, really, but it was more than some people had.

So that was why, when I saw the empty space where my backpack was supposed to be, I came to a halt right in the middle of the room. My hands began to shake.

"Where is it?"

My inquiry seemed lost in the space. I could hear other voices coming from upstairs. Clutching my rapidly heating hands into fists, I whirled around and stormed for the staircase. I took the steps two at a time and followed the sound of the voices until they stopped. But I already knew where they were. I threw my hand against the door, causing an ooze of pink energy to splatter against the hard surface. Two girls—younger ones, and new arrivals—looked up, their expressions morphing from surprise to alarm.

"What the hell?" I said, spying my backpack sitting beside the smaller of the two. She at least had the decency to look guilty as I fixed her with a furious glare. "Is this what you do where you're from? Steal the belongings of the people who gave you a place to sleep?"

"You didn't give us anything," the other girl said, causing me to whip my head in her direction. Her gaze flicked to my hand, which was still pressed against the door. I could feel the energy coursing over my fingers like warm water over winter-chilled skin.

"Excuse me?"

"This is Ayla's house."

"It's nobody's house," I said, nearly spitting the words. I pulled my hand into a fist, carefully removing it from the door at the same time. "And it's everybody's. If you think you can just come in here and take my stuff, you—"

"If it's everybody's house, it's everybody's stuff."

I just stared at her, feeling like my eyes were going to pop out of my head. *Who the hell does this kid think she is, anyway?*

"Bennie, come on." The smaller girl started to stand up, but the little bitch—Bennie, apparently— grabbed her wrist.

"No. Sit down. Just because some bitchy old lady can't share her stuff doesn't mean the code doesn't still apply."

I couldn't help the laugh that burst out of me. "Old lady? I'm twenty."

"Hag."

Both of my hands flared so suddenly that it startled me. It startled the girls, too, and they leaped to their feet. But, still clutched in Bennie's hand . . .

"That's *mine*," I said, my voice a low growl.

"Yeah?" She peered at the framed photo, studying it with feigned interest. "Your parents are *old*. Were they, like, sixty when they adopted you from China?"

I didn't owe the little brat any explanation at all. But I couldn't stand the way she was smirking, waiting for me to take the bait. "Can I have that back now?"

"So, which one of them was sterile?"

"Neither of them, you little shit. Those are my grandparents. My mom was white." I tried to cool the fire in my voice, but I could tell I'd failed when Bennie's smirk settled into a little smile of victory. "Do you really want a picture of some Rifter and her grandparents?" I asked. She stared at me for a moment, looked at the photo, and then casually tossed it toward me. Well, sort of toward me. I didn't have any hope of catching it, and I knew what the result was going to be even before I saw the corner of the frame hit the hard floor. The crack of glass reverberated like a gunshot in the small bedroom, and both girls jumped. The smaller one began to cry.

"I'm sorry!" she wailed, her gaze pleading. Bennie turned to her in disbelief.

"Don't apologize! She's pointing pinkhands at you!"

I realized I was standing there shaking, both hands raised, glowing palms aimed directly at the girls.

"That's exactly when you should apologize!" the smaller girl cried. She turned back to me. "We won't do it again."

"Damn right, you won't," I said. My gaze drifted down to the frame lying face down on the floor. Slowly, I lowered my hands.

Bennie leaned closer to her friend. "Grab the stuff," she whispered, keeping her gaze defiantly on me.

"You looking to die today?"

She laughed. "You're full of it. If you really did go around killing people for worthless crap, you would've been exed already."

"Not if I were under the protection of a ruthless boss."

"Yeah? Are you?"

"Probably better for you if you don't know."

She snorted. "That's what I thought." She bent down, grabbed my backpack, and started to stuff my meagre belongings back into it. But she left the frame on the floor. When she was done, she zipped up the bag, slung it over her shoulder, and grabbed her friend's arm. "We're leaving now."

"Oh, yeah, you are. When Ayla finds out that you're a couple of little thieves, she'll probably report you to Joshua. And I'll be giving her some suggestions for what to say. So you better run."

The smaller girl's tears, which had tapered off a little, began to flow again. "Bennie! We just found this place. Give her back her stuff."

"Are you kidding? Do you know how hard it is to find decent boots around here? Reusable pads? Any kind of pads?"

"They give those out at the checkpoints."

Bennie sighed, as if she were already tired of having to explain things. "When's the last time you ever got anything from a checkpoint? The bosses take everything, idiot."

"Nice friend you are," I muttered. Bennie glared at me, clutching the strap of the backpack in one hand and her friend's arm in the other.

"Probably better than you. Now, move."

"You're not taking my stuff."

"Yeah?" She let go of the strap and raised her hand. A flare of pink exploded around her fingers in unison with the flare of panic in my heart. "You really wanna do this?"

I did not. Some worn-out clothes, a pair of stinky

boots, the dull scissors I used to chew my stupidly straight hair into the approximation of a bob, and some reusable pads (which were kind of unnecessary since I hadn't had a period in months) were hardly worth dying over. It was the principle of the thing . . . but what good were principles now?

So I stepped away from the door, watching warily as Bennie and her friend edged past me. As soon as they were out of view, I heard them break into a run and thunder down the stairs. With a sigh, I looked down at the frame, then bent to pick it up.

A crack ran all the way through the glass, diagonally from one side to the other, bisecting the photo of me and my grandparents. Young and old. Rifter and untouched. Alive and dead.

With shaking hands, I managed to get the photo out from behind the broken glass. I folded it in half and stuck it in my other jacket pocket, far away from Joshua's stupid map.

CHAPTER 3

OPEN HOUSE

Maybe losing my stuff was for the best, I thought as I trudged east, unburdened by the remnants of my past. The backpack might've been a liability, anyway, making it more difficult to squeeze into tight spaces and potentially giving assailants something to grab. Still, I felt a bit naked as I walked, realizing that what I had on me was all I had left in the world. That vulnerable sensation kind of made me want to stuff my hands into my jacket pockets, but I kept them out, just in case. I might not have looked like I had anything to steal . . . but I didn't want to take any chances, especially since I was about to walk onto another boss' territory.

Edging past the overgrown lilac bushes on the corner of Havilland and Monroe, I held my breath. Not because of the smell (it was lovely), but because you never knew when Lex would start barking. The house on the corner remained quiet, though, and when I tiptoed past the front porch, I glanced up and saw that the front door was open, swinging in the lazy spring air.

I stopped for a moment, staring at the sight. The neon-pink occupancy ticket was still nailed to the door. Tattered as it was, it marked a place where life existed. A place that was—at least to those who honoured the unofficial code—off limits.

My stomach's first instinct was to growl. On any other day, that would've gotten Lex's sharp ears twitching, and I would've been on the receiving end of a different kind of growl. But the house remained quiet, and no scruffy white nuisance appeared at the door.

My stomach's second instinct was to clench, and I almost let out a groan. "All right, all right," I muttered, my heart picking up its pace as I stepped toward the porch and its four steps. The inside of the house looked dark, but that didn't mean much since it was the middle of a sunny afternoon. There wasn't much need for lamps.

The house was right on the border of Joshua's turf. I wasn't entirely sure who would try to call dibs if, in fact, the place had been abandoned. Mind you, an abandoned house didn't always mean a good haul. Sometimes people packed up all the good stuff and took it with them.

Sometimes they just died, though, and left a stinking mess.

What if Lex ate them? I wondered, then shook my head. It was unlikely. If he were alive enough to snack on his owner, he would've been out there barking at me. No, the house had been abandoned . . . either by relocation or death. I wasn't sure if I really wanted to find out which.

Glancing around, I listened for voices and footsteps. The street was quiet. Slowly, I climbed the steps, my hand on the splintery wooden railing. My sneakers, even with their soft soles, sounded loud. When I reached the top and brushed off my hands, I stepped closer to the open door and peered inside.

"Hello?" I whispered, expecting to hear a frenzy of barking at any moment. My muscles tensed in anticipation. But there was nothing to answer my greeting. "Hello? Lex?" Calling the dog felt silly, but I didn't know his owner's name. The only reason I knew *his* was because I'd heard someone cursing at the dog on more than one occasion.

But no angry dog appeared to bark. No angry owner appeared to chase me off their porch. Bracing one hand on the doorframe, I leaned inside and took a deep breath in through my nose. I didn't smell anything, but that didn't mean much. If they'd died upstairs—and recently—there might not've been much to smell.

A part of me really wanted to explore the house. But I'd already taken the job from Joshua, and he demanded quick results. And follow-through. If I didn't show up with either the loot or an excuse, he'd be coming for me.

Still, I couldn't just leave a potential treasure trove like that, could I? So I reached out and pulled the door closed, careful to make sure it latched. I smoothed down the pink ticket, making sure it was still affixed solidly to the door (it was) and that it wasn't about to go flying off with a strong gust of wind (it wasn't . . . but the air was so still, that was hardly a concern). Then, with a last glance of anticipation at the empty house, I hurried down the steps and back to the street.

—

I hadn't been on Niesha's turf much since the Rift. I'd passed through it many times with Grandpa—before—on the way to the mall over in Hurstleigh, but the main road kind of bypassed the tree-lined streets with all the pretty houses. I hadn't known anyone who'd lived there.

The area appeared to have been haphazardly abandoned. Most of the lawns were overgrown, as were the flowering shrubs on some of the properties. But the whole area still looked a hell of a lot nicer than where I had been living.

I walked slowly, checking out the houses as if I were simply a sightseer on a walking tour of the neighbourhood. Grandpa's house had been nice . . . but pretty damn modest compared to the houses I saw around me. These things probably had luxury en suites with jetted tubs and steam showers and heated tile floors. They probably had spacious kitchens, too, with huge fridges that offered more room than one family could ever need. And pantries full of food. My heart skipped a little as my mouth began to water and my stomach let out another growl. My head understood what my body didn't, though; any food that might've been left behind by the original owners was long gone, either eaten or rotten.

It was hard to see the numbers on some of the houses since the greenery was so overgrown. I was looking for 145 Cherry Lane, and I almost missed it. 149 Cherry Lane stared me in the face, the numbers smeared with dusty-looking verdigris on a porch post. Swivelling on my heel, I marched back the way I'd come.

I didn't see the house number until I was standing at the bottom of the porch steps, staring up into the shadows. A large rhododendron was growing out of control, destroying any sort of view the former home-owners might've had from their front porch. The numbers were right beside the door, black against the white-shingle siding. My gaze flicked over to the door itself, which was bright red. Clashing mightily with the crimson surface was a pink ticket.

Officially occupied. Great. I didn't know if Joshua knew about that or not. Probably. The whole thing was most likely an impossible errand, and he was sitting back there on his throne at that very moment, laughing over how utterly stupid hungry people could be.

Yeah, well, hunger could make people do stupid things . . . like walk into a ticketed house in the middle of the day to try to steal a bunch of snacks and recreational drugs. I reached out and placed my hand on the doorknob, holding my breath. When nothing happened, I turned the knob.

Locked. Of course it was. I let go of the knob and edged sideways toward the window. The sheer curtains were drawn, but thanks to the shadow of the bush behind me, I could sort of see inside. There were no movements or shadows within. In fact, I could see all the way through to the windows at the back of the house.

Open concept, I thought. *Must be nice.* My grandparents' house had been old, sort of a twisty collection of tiny rooms and cramped spaces. I'd bashed my elbow on the bathroom doorframe more times than I cared to count. And yet, in a strange way, I missed that old house and my aching funny bone.

The window wasn't the sort that opened, so I moved along the porch until I got to a bit that wrapped around the side of the house. I peered around the corner and spotted another window . . . and, this time, it *was* the kind that opened. Tiptoeing (for once grateful that I wasn't wearing my boots), I made my way closer. The latch was on the inside. Luckily, though, I didn't have to worry about that; the window itself was open about an inch.

I slipped my fingers into the space, my heart pounding. *Get a grip. It's not a guillotine.* Wincing at the slight squeak as I pulled the window upward, I strained to listen. Still nothing. It wouldn't have been uncommon for a cache house to be left unattended. They were all over the place, their locations known mostly to the bosses and their lackeys. But leaving a cache house unattended with an open window was just reckless.

Either that, or it was a trap.

I paused in front of the window, which I'd gotten open far enough that I could climb through it if I wanted to. But I wasn't sure I did. There had to be an easier way to earn a can of beans. Maybe Niesha had some jobs I could do. If I ripped her off now, though . . .

In the end, my stomach made the decision for me. I was beyond thinking clearly. So I slipped my leg through the window, ducked down, and slid into the house.

The floor under the window was a bit dirty, which seemed to suggest it had been open for a while. A new thought occurred to me. *Maybe there's no stash here at all. Joshua could've been messing with you. After all, why would he send some random girl who walks in off the street to get his snacks and weed? Wouldn't that be a job for someone he, you know, trusted?*

I had no idea what to think anymore. My stomach was making it hard to think about anything. I slipped through the space, heading for the kitchen. My sneakers sounded ridiculously loud on the dusty hardwood. As I rounded the corner and stepped into the sprawling room, I sucked in a little gasp.

As I'd suspected, the fridge was big. Like, not even large. *Huge.* It was probably twice the width of Grandpa's, and well over six feet high. I hurried over and grasped the sleek handle. I could just barely hear the thing humming, unlike Grandpa's fridge, which had rattled and buzzed with each defrost cycle. But when I yanked the door open, all thoughts of gourmet meals and a full belly fled on a tsunami of disappointment.

The damn thing was empty.

I let the door close on its own and turned away with a sigh, only to startle a moment later as I heard a small thump. My hands flared, and I caught a glimpse of pink out of the corner of my eye.

Jumpy, much? That was just your reflection in the fridge door.

Clenching my fists so tightly they shot out a few juicy-pink sparks, I tiptoed through the attached space—probably once a family room with a big TV; all that was left were a few wires sticking out of the wall—and headed for the staircase. Logically, snacks would've been in the kitchen. But if you were trying to hide them from hungry scavengers, that was probably a stupid choice of hiding spot.

The stairs made a ridiculous amount of noise as I

made my way to the second floor, at least to my own ramped-up ears. I could almost hear the creak of individual nails in the house's framing, the slow breakdown of wood as the house aged. The air seemed to sing, and not just because I was carrying a pretty high voltage in my sweaty hands. Pausing for a moment at the top of the stairs, I took the opportunity to take a few deep breaths and shake off the glow. Pinkhands might've been a good deterrent, but they were also a danger to me. I didn't particularly want any more burns on my thighs.

The ceiling was pretty high, and, as I peered down into the foyer below, I could hear my own nervous breath echoing back at me. Running one hand over the smooth railing, I walked slowly down the spacious hallway, heading for the room at the end. It wasn't likely there were any beds—after all, I hadn't seen any furniture yet—but I did kind of want to see the bathroom while I was there. How often did someone like me get to go poking around in a house like that? Joshua's job was most likely a bust, so I had a few minutes to explore.

The room at the end of the hall was huge and, as I expected, empty. There had been a bed at one point; the divots were still in the plush area rug (which, for some reason, had been left behind). Feeling deliciously silly, I slipped off my shoes and padded over in my bare feet, positioning myself under the glittering chandelier. It almost felt like curling my toes into a dog's fur, something I hadn't done in years. Frankly, I was glad Floyd had died before things had all gone to shit. I didn't think I could've handled watching what had happened to so many of the other dogs in town happen to him.

My gaze drifted down to my feet, landing on the missing baby toe of my right foot. With a sigh, I looked over at my shoes. It seemed I couldn't even enjoy going barefoot anymore.

Regretfully, I walked back to my shoes, spying the half-open door to the bathroom as I did so. *Just a quick peek*, I thought. *Then I'm out of here.* I slipped over to the door and pushed it open. The hinges let out a bit of a squeak, then fell silent. I stepped into the space and spotted the switches on the wall next to the door. I had no idea what they all did, but I figured one of them might've been for the in-floor heating I suspected was under those shiny marble tiles. *Just for a second*, I thought, reaching out for the most promising switch. *Just to see what it's like.*

But my fingers never even touched the switch. The next instant, something slammed into me, sending me sprawling toward the toilet. My hands flared, pink blurs flailing as I reached out to stop my fall. The sound of the bathroom door slamming shut barely registered. The only thing I could concentrate on was the strong hand that grabbed me by the back of my jacket and threw me sideways into the huge shower.

CHAPTER 4

NOT-SO-DYNAMIC DUO

I probably should've screamed or something, but I was too freaked out. Besides, there was no one around to hear. No one except the two figures with me in the shadowy bathroom. Careful not to make any sudden moves, I sort of rolled against the wall, my shoulder letting me know I was going to have some lovely bruises later. The groan escaped before I could stop it.

"Sorry! Sorry, sorry," a voice said, and it took a moment for me to put the pieces together and realize that the person who'd just thrown me against a hard tile wall was, for some reason, apologizing. "Are you okay?"

"Do I look okay?" I snapped, raising my hands instinctively. They were still glowing bright pink . . . and the glow illuminated the concerned face of the guy crouching in front of me. Well, half of it looked concerned. The other half was kind of a mess, the cheek scarred and lumpy. One eye was cloudy, probably the result of whatever it was that had happened to his face. His other eye inspected me from under a brow twisted in a frown. I could see the pink glow of my hands reflected back at me in its dark surface.

"Could you turn those things off?" he asked.

"Yeah, right. Some guy tackles me into a shower stall, and I'm supposed to let down my only defence?"

He rolled his eyes. The light was getting a little dimmer as the day waned, but I could still see well enough to see that. "I didn't *tackle* you. You think I go around tackling random women?"

"How should I know? I don't even know who the hell you are."

"Viktor," he said, as if that should've explained everything.

"Yeah? Well, *Viktor*, you threw me in here, so—"

"I was trying to stop you from doing a header into the toilet." He shook his head and stood up. From my perspective, huddled on the bottom of the shower, he looked intimidatingly tall. As he held out his hand, I shrank back against the tiles. "Come on. I don't bite."

"Everybody bites," I said, raising my hands a little more. I kept my fingers straight, hoping to emphasize the power running over my skin.

"Not *everybody*, if we're being technical."

"Yeah, well, you're in the demographic. Rifter."

He snorted. "Says the Rifter."

"Back off."

He did—a little—and my taut muscles started to unclench. I gave my trembling hands a shake as I blew out a long breath. Viktor's mismatched gaze fixed on the pink splashes for a moment before sinking down to my foot.

"What happened to your toe?" he asked.

"What happened to your face?" I shot right back at him. For a moment, something flashed across his features, visible even in the meagre light. But it was gone just as quickly as it had come. He reached back and tightened his ponytail with a quick tug.

"I'm not actually in the habit of telling my life story to complete strangers. I don't even know your name."

"You don't need to know it." With a grunt, I rubbed my shoulder. "You didn't have to throw me in here so hard."

"I was trying to stop you from hitting the toilet."

I stared up at him in disbelief. "I wouldn't have been heading for the toilet at all if you hadn't body-slammed me!"

"That was an accident."

"Uh-huh."

"It was." He looked back at the other figure, who I'd totally forgotten about. The kid was just standing there beside the closed door, watching and listening. Quietly. Whereas Viktor was tall and dark and reminded me of an inexplicably suntanned vampire, this other guy was short and . . . well, sort of golden. His skin was a warm beige, and his curls were almost blond. I couldn't really see the colour of his eyes in the miserable lighting, but they weren't dark. "I sort of lost my balance when I reached out," Viktor said, turning back to me.

"Why were you groping at me in the first place?"

"You were about to turn on the light."

"Huh?"

"The light." He nodded up at the fixture on the ceiling. "It's how we signal."

"Signal?" I repeated, twisting around to look up. Above the tiles at the top of the wall was a shallow window.

"Yeah."

"To who?"

"One of the other caches."

I stood up carefully, bracing one hand on the smooth tiles. "I wasn't reaching for the light switch."

"Um, yeah, you were. I saw you."

"Forget it." I took a step forward before realizing my path out of there was blocked. Not just by the closed door, but by the two guys standing in front of it. My fists tightened at my sides. Viktor's sharp gaze immediately stuck there.

"Come on. There's no need to bring out the hand farts."

Despite my fear, I nearly choked on a laugh. "The what?"

"You know." He raised his hands one at a time, each movement accompanied by the brief blowing of a raspberry. My eyes widened at the sight of the hot- pink energy coursing over his skin. I took a step back, and he quickly shook his hands as if trying to rid them of excess water. "Sorry."

"Can I go?" I asked, trying to still the tremble in my voice. "Or am I your prisoner?"

"Prisoner?" His left eyebrow rose over the cloudy eye. "Seriously?" With a sweeping motion, he stepped aside and reached for the doorknob. The other guy scrambled out of the way without a word. "Go, then."

"What's the catch?" I asked, perhaps stupidly. But something about this didn't seem right. I'd spent the last two years fighting for every scrap, getting bruised and burned in the process, learning to depend only on myself and guard against my yearning to trust some-one my own age. Viktor didn't fit into my perception of the world since the Rift; he might as well have been dropped into it from another dimension.

"No catch. Less paperwork for us if you just leave now." He waved his hand out the door. But I didn't move.

"Paperwork?"

"Not really."

"No shit."

He seemed to bristle a little. "You didn't steal anything, did you?"

"No."

"Well, then, there's nothing to report. We'll just forget we ever saw you." His hand was still pointing out the door. But now my mind was racing. *Steal? Steal what? Is there stuff to steal? Maybe if you hadn't been so obsessed with heated floors, you could've found something before these two stopped you.*

The thought was almost more than I could bear. As if commiserating, my stomach let out a huge growl. I took a step back and sank down onto the closed toilet seat, defeated.

"Um . . ." Viktor began. I curled my arms around my middle and bent over.

"Go away."

"Are you okay?"

I bowed my head, letting my roughly cut hair swing forward to hide my face. The sound of Viktor's footsteps registered as he abandoned the door and came closer. But I didn't even have the strength to throw up pinkhands in warning.

"Hey." The gentleness in his voice made me look up to find him crouched in front of me. "We don't want anything from you. You can go. It's fine."

"It's *not* fine," I said miserably. "If I don't get what I came for, I don't get paid."

"By who?"

"I'm not telling you that. You could be working for Permanent Marc for all I know."

"How do I know *you* aren't working for him?"

"Wouldn't you know it if we worked for the same boss?"

"Exactly. So you're working for someone else and trying to throw me off. So, who is it? C-Roy? Rasputin? King Joshua?"

"King Joshua? Who the hell calls him that?"

"Niesha. I suspect she's being facetious."

"He's hardly a king. Just because someone builds himself a throne out of an old recliner doesn't make him a king."

"So you're working for him."

"And you're working for Niesha. Glad we got that out of the way." I pulled my arms tighter around myself. "Now do we have to duel to the death or something?"

"That would hardly be a fair fight. How would it look if a guy like me challenged a starving girl to a duel?"

"I'm not starving," I snapped, the lie echoing a little in the darkening room. "Besides, I'm sure I could take a half-blind asshole."

"Dang. I'd hate to see how you treat your *real* enemies. But I'm just going to chalk that up to you being hangry." Hesitantly, he reached out and touched my knee. My gaze fixed on his fingers, which were—thankfully—not aglow at that moment. "If you want a proxy duel, we can do that. But let's get something to eat first, okay? I wouldn't feel right fighting someone who looks like she's about to pass out."

CHAPTER 5

AN EVENING STROLL

I wasn't about to walk in front of two random guys that I'd met while trying to steal from their boss. But they were quick as they made their way through the sunset-lit neighbourhood, and I found myself having to jog to keep up. Viktor had long legs, so his pace wasn't surprising. But his companion was a lot shorter—shorter than me, actually—and he had this weird, bouncy gait that almost made it look like he was wearing spring-loaded shoes. He wasn't, though. He wore a pair of rustic sandals over mismatched socks. That was hardly the weirdest part of his outfit. Aside from the denim jacket and jeans, he had on what looked like some sort of costume. His shirt was a blousy thing with beading around the front placket. This was tucked into . . . well, a skirt. Some sort of swingy, gathered garment that seemed kind of unnecessary, given the jeans underneath.

Viktor led us along the sidewalks in silence, then cut down a path that ran between two fences and emerged onto a lane crowded with overturned recycling bins. Whatever had been in them was long gone. He edged one of them aside with his foot to clear access to another path. His golden friend scampered down it while he stood there, looking at me. I shuffled to a stop.

"What?" I asked.

"Nothing." His mismatched gaze landed on my shoes. I looked down, wondering what he was looking at. "It's weird, though, isn't it?"

"What is?"

"Well," he said slowly, waving his hand like he wanted me to walk ahead of him down the path. When I didn't budge, he shrugged and started after his friend. I followed, hoping he would slow down a bit if he wanted to have a conversation. "Here we are."

"You going to get to the point?"

He chuckled and glanced back at me over his shoulder. "It's just that, when I take a girl out for dinner, I usually know her name."

"This isn't a date," I snapped. "I don't even know you."

"I'm Viktor."

"Yeah, you said that. But I don't know who or what you are. Other than annoying," I finished under my breath. But he must've heard me because he let out a grunt of laughter.

"So I've been told." He turned around and walked backward. "Viktor Knowles. Seventeen years old.

Tragic orphan dependent upon the kindness of extended family. One of the original Rifters."

"You were in the school?"

"Yeah. Weren't you?"

"Don't you think you would recognize me if we had gone to the same high school?"

He shrugged. "I guess. Homeschooled?"

"None of your business."

"Private school?"

I snorted. "Do I look rich to you?"

"Hard to tell. The Rift was a great equalizer."

I frowned at the lumpy scars on the left side of his face. "Did the Rift do that?"

"What?"

"Melt your face."

"In a way." He turned back around and walked a little faster. With a sigh, I jogged to catch up.

"Where are we going? Isn't there any food back at your house?"

"Nothing I'd want to feed someone like you."

I gaped at him. Being on his left side with that cloudy eye, though, I wasn't sure if he even noticed. "What's that supposed to mean? Someone like me?"

"You look *really* hungry. I don't think a bag of Cheeznudles is going to do it."

So there *was* junk food in there. Damn it.

"I make a mean marinara."

"With what? Ketchup?"

He snorted. "Is that your idea of fine dining?"

"Look, I don't know who you are—"

"Viktor."

"—or what kind of scam you're running, but—"

"Scam?" He came to a halt so quickly that I went a few more paces before I was able to stop myself. "Why would I scam you?"

"Are you serious? Have you been living here for the past three years?"

"Three years, two months, and fourteen days."

"Keeping track?"

"Yeah. In my planner. It has kittens on it."

I scrutinized his face, trying to suss out any sort of humour. It wasn't hard. The undamaged side twitched as if he were trying really hard not to smile.

"Kittens," I said.

"Pink ones. Rift kittens."

I narrowed my eyes.

"Sorry. I forgot what I was dealing with."

"What's that?"

"A hangry woman."

I was beyond hangry. Somewhere around the time my period had stopped, I'd gone from hangry to . . . well, defeated. Anger required more energy than I had. Although, it did still come in quick, unsustainable bursts. And Viktor was doing a good job of drawing those out.

Before I could say anything, though, he tilted his chin at something behind me. "Go on," he said. "It's just up there."

I turned to look but couldn't figure out what he meant. His companion was gone, and all I could see was the lane between two stone fences stretching before us. The shadows were deepening, especially where trees hung over the fences on either side. Snatches of gold from the setting sun blinked through the leaves.

"Come on," Viktor said, suddenly at my side. I felt his fingers on my elbow, and I jerked away. My hands flashed pink. I whipped them behind my back, hoping he hadn't seen. He ignored my recoil and marched toward an opening in the fence on the right. As I got closer, I could see it was an open gate. The yard beyond was full of overgrown bushes and shrubs, and the grass was halfway to my knees, which made it look like some sort of weird suburban jungle. As I stepped inside and looked up at the house, Viktor closed the gate.

"Who lives here?" I asked, my gaze fixing on the warm glow of the illuminated windows. The sheer curtains were drawn, so I couldn't see inside clearly. What I could see, though, were a couple of dark shapes moving within like shadow puppets. Viktor let out a quick grunt of laughter.

"Are you serious? Who do you think lives here?"

I turned to him with a frown. "How should I know?"

He shook his head and headed for the porch steps. "I'll chalk this up to your brain needing fuel."

The organ in question stuttered and spun as I tried to make sense of his words. The answer hit me like a lead safe to the foot.

CHAPTER 6

FINE DINING

There were plenty of things you didn't do in the Rift Zone. One of them—and a pretty big one at that—was fraternize with one boss while you were doing a job for another. That sort of thing, even if done innocently enough, usually led to suspicions and accusations and . . . well, the whipping-out of pinkhands for some sort of punishment.

But the sun had almost disappeared, and I was in unfamiliar territory. I wasn't sure if I could find my way back to Ayla's place from there in the dark, and, besides, doing so would've meant going through quite a bit of enemy territory.

Suck it up, I told myself. *You do what you have to do. If there's food here, you eat. How's Joshua ever going to know?*

Viktor was waiting at the back door. With a last glance at the gate (and hoping I was making the right choice), I slowly climbed the steps.

"Whew. Wasn't sure if you were going to make it."

"Shut up."

He held up his hands. "I'm just saying. I'm impressed you're able to walk at all."

I frowned. "I'm not *that* skinny."

"It's not that." He tilted his head as he regarded me. "It's more of a . . . hunger."

"No shit."

"I'm not surprised. That kind of requires food."

I just narrowed my eyes at him as he waited for me to respond to his stupid joke. But all he did was sigh.

"Come on," he said, grasping the doorknob. "There's enough for one more."

The smell that hit me when he opened that door almost made my knees buckle. I hadn't smelled anything so heavenly in years. Not since the last time I'd baked a batch of cookies. As I stepped into the warmly lit space, drawn by the mind-numbing aroma, I briefly wondered if I'd died and this was all some sort of afterlife dream.

The room I found myself standing in was a kitchen. It was smaller than the one in Viktor's house, but still pretty impressive. And clean.

"Shoes off," the young woman at the stove said without even bothering to turn around. I looked down and spied the golden boy's sandals on the doormat, pointed neatly toward the wall. He'd parked himself on one of the stools at the large island; his toes barely touched the rungs. Viktor bent down to untie the laces on his black boots.

"She's serious," he whispered to me. "You get her floors dirty, there'll be heck to pay."

After a moment of hesitation, I slipped off my shoes. Now was not the time for vanity. Besides, Viktor and his friend had already seen my non-existent toe.

When our shoes were off, Viktor led me over to the island. I climbed onto the stool between the two guys, marvelling at the cleanliness of the surface in front of me. The white quartz sparkled in the light from the three pendant lamps that hung above us. It was the sort of countertop Grandma had always dreamed of, back before she'd gotten sick and her renovation plans had been put on hold. Slowly, I reached out and pressed my shaking hands on the stone. It was deliciously cool.

"So," the woman said, finally turning around to face us. If she was surprised by my presence, she didn't let it show. She just stepped closer, holding one hand under the bowl of a wooden spoon that appeared to be full of a creamy sauce. "Does this need anything?" she asked Viktor, who leaned on the island to sample the offering. He smacked his lips dramatically as he sank back on his seat.

"Lemon juice?"

"You going to find me a lemon?"

He chuckled. "Tastes okay to me."

"Good. Because it's the best I can do. I used the last of the salt in the cookies."

"Cookies?" I squeaked. The word just sort of

popped out before I could stop it. The woman smiled and turned to set the spoon in the sink.

"Oatmeal raisin."

Viktor sighed. "Raisins."

"If you want chocolate chips, find me some."

"The checkpoints haven't given those out in years."

"And you think I can make them appear out of thin air or something?" She turned down the heat on the sauce pot. "Are you staying for dinner?"

"Um, yeah," Viktor said. "Why else would we—"

"I wasn't talking to you." She turned back to us and fixed her gaze on me. "Well?"

"Can I?"

Her full lips twisted in amusement. I couldn't quite tell how old she was. Maybe a little older than me. Her black curls were pulled back in a fluffy ponytail, and her eyes were almost as dark as Viktor's. Her skin was a rich brown, which only highlighted the large pink scar on her left elbow. When she spotted where my gaze had landed, she looked down there herself.

"Badge of honour," she said, turning her gaze back to meet mine. "Hurt like a bitch, though."

"And made you a mortal enemy," Viktor added. "Where are the cookies?"

"What are you? Five?"

"No, I'm Viktor. And I want cookies."

The woman snorted. "He's Viktor, all right," she said to me, a twinkle in her eyes as if she were sharing a secret. "I'm Niesha."

"*You're* Niesha?"

She seemed taken aback. "Yeah. Why? What were you expecting?"

I wasn't sure how to answer that question. Bosses always turned out to be a lot less impressive than their stories built them up to be. But until you actually met one, they were sort of these mythical figures. Almost gods. And in our town in the post-Rift world . . . they pretty much were.

"Six feet tall," Viktor said, jarring me out of my musings. "Battle cry of a banshee. Pinkhands that can slay an army of zitty kids at fifty paces. A body to die for."

"Cool it. That's *your* fantasy." Niesha rolled her eyes before turning back to me. "I'm just a regular person, trying to live my life in this crazy town. Just like everyone else."

"Excuse me," Viktor said. "Since when am I regular?" He nudged my arm with the back of his hand, causing me to startle. Thankfully, it wasn't enough to cause my hands to flare. "You going to tell Niesha your name? Or do we just make something up?"

"Jesus," Niesha said. "Don't let him do that. You better give us a name."

I chewed on my lip for a moment. I could've easily given them a fake name. That would've been the safest thing to do. Especially if word got back to Joshua. But I was too tired to care much anymore.

"What about . . ." Viktor began, but I shook my head.

"Léa."

"Really?" he said, his voice dripping with disbelief. I turned to him with a frown.

"What's wrong with it?"

"Nothing. You just don't *look* like a Léa."

"What do I look like, then?"

He leaned back on his stool a little, as if trying to get a better look at me. In the brighter light of the kitchen, I could clearly see the awful scarring on his face. Stiff, raised channels of pink tissue ran from his jawline all the way up to his lower eyelid, which I noticed didn't have all of its eyelashes. The eye itself looked like it was covered in a cloudy contact lens; I doubted he could see much out of it at all.

"She looks hungry," Niesha said, drawing our attention back to her. "I was just about to get the pasta started."

"Pasta again?" Viktor said, his voice almost a whine.

"You find something else, and I'll cook it."

"You find us a good lead, and I will."

"I've got one," I said, the words popping out before I could stop myself. Viktor and Niesha both looked at me. I shrank back a little. "Maybe. It might be nothing, but—"

"Where?" Niesha asked.

"Havilland and Monroe."

She frowned. "King Joshua's turf?"

"He's not a king," I snapped. "And he probably doesn't even know about it. I found it today. It *was* ticketed, but—"

"Was?"

"I think they're . . . gone. Recently, though."

With a nod, she turned and bent down. When she straightened back up, she had a pot in her hands. She proceeded to fill it at the sink. "We'll check it out," she said, raising her voice to be heard over the water. "In the meantime, let's eat before Viktor starts whining again."

"Hey! I don't do that." His voice was an exaggerated whine. Niesha smiled and put the pot on the stove to boil.

—

The forkful of saucy spaghetti on the plate in front of me was disappointing . . . and it must've shown on my face.

"Start with that," Niesha said. Since there were only three stools, she stood on the other side of the island behind her own plate, which, in comparison to mine, seemed positively piled with pasta. "If you haven't eaten in a while, you'll make yourself sick if you overdo it."

"It'll come out both ends," Viktor said around a mouthful of hanging noodles. He sucked them up with a noisy slurp.

"Gross," Niesha said. "But true. And you don't want to waste that. Your body needs it."

I sighed and turned back to my "meal." I ignored

the fork and plucked at the pile with my fingers, snagging a single noodle. Maybe, if I ate them one at a time, it would seem like more than it was.

"Should we check out that place tomorrow?" Viktor asked. Niesha nodded.

"Léa can show us the way." She ate a large forkful of spaghetti that she'd twirled onto her fork and chewed thoughtfully. "Is the king going to be a problem?"

"He's not a king," I said, reaching for another noodle. "Don't inflate his ego. And he shouldn't be a problem. I didn't tell him about the house. I didn't even find it until I was on my way over here."

"On a job?"

The noodles were slippery. I remained silent as I tried to grab another, still chewing on the one I had in my mouth.

"It's fine. We all do what we have to."

I abandoned the noodles for a moment and looked up at her. "What kind of attitude is that for a boss?"

"I never asked to be a boss. I'm just trying to keep things organized on this side of town. If people want to bestow me with some sort of honorary title, that's their prerogative." She twirled more spaghetti onto her fork.

"Yeah, but doesn't it piss you off when people try to steal your stashes?"

Her eyebrows rose. "People like you?"

"I guess."

"You're hungry, aren't you?"

"Yeah."

"Yeah, so, I can see why you'd take a job. Any job." She shook her head. "And if it's Joshua we're talking about here, you were probably looking for some pretty stupid shit. Am I right?"

"Let me guess," Viktor said, setting his fork down on his empty plate. "Condoms. Vape pens. Beer. The true necessities of life."

"Joshua's had it too easy for too long," Niesha said. "If you have the luxury of worrying about that shit, you're doing pretty well for yourself."

"So you don't have any of that?" I asked, wondering whether she'd even answer me. To my surprise, though, she smiled.

"Of course. I just don't worry about it. It's currency. Nothing more. If I have the choice between a stash full of that crap and a stash full of food that people can actually eat, guess which one I'm going to pick."

I shook my head and turned my focus back to the noodles in front of me. "You're not like any boss I've ever met."

"Yeah. Lucky for you. Because any other boss probably would've tossed you out by now. Or given you another scar for your collection."

I curled my toes up tight, even though she couldn't see them from where she was standing. "Is that what happened to you?" I asked, casting a quick glance at Viktor.

"Yeah. Terrible business. One of them caught me

when I was trying to steal a planner. You know, the one with Rift kittens on it."

Niesha snorted and shook her head. But she didn't say anything.

"Threw a pinkball right at my face! I thought I was going to die. But at least I got the planner."

"Are you done?" Niesha asked.

"Maybe. Oh, wait! No, I haven't told her about what they did when I tried to steal a pen so I could write in the planner. But I can't show you *that*," he said to me with a wicked grin, "because I don't show anybody what's down—"

"Okay, okay." Niesha reached for his empty plate and stacked it with her own. "So you're a comedian tonight?"

He sucked in a gasp. "You think my hideous scars are *funny?*"

She turned to me with a roll of her eyes. "You'll get used to it."

"What?"

"That." She waved her hand in Viktor's direction. He was sitting there with this pained expression . . . which was sort of wobbly. A moment later, his face exploded into a smile.

"Gotta keep things light," he said, "'cause the truth is so stupid."

"And what's the truth?" I asked.

"He did it to himself." Niesha folded her arms and raised her eyebrows.

"On purpose?"

Viktor snorted. "Why would I do that?"

"I don't know," I said. "You're kind of weird."

He placed his hand on his chest. "Thank you."

"So, how did it happen?"

"It was during . . . the Week of Alarm." His voice took on a dramatic tone.

"The *what?*"

Niesha shook her head. "A few months after the evacuation. Most people had left town. It was supposed to be temporary, remember? So they set their house alarms. When the Rifters started getting desperate, what did they do?"

"Broke into houses," I said, suddenly understanding.

"On this side of town, it was crazy loud for about a week. Those things were going off all the time. I don't think any of us got much sleep."

I turned to Viktor. "What does that have to do with your face?"

"Okay. Combine a guy with a strong startle reflex and random screaming alarms, and . . ."

"You don't have a strong startle reflex."

"I did back then. Before I started meditating."

I snorted, thinking he was joking. But I couldn't detect any twitches of mirth on the undamaged side of his face. "How does a startle reflex lead to—"

"I was in the middle of shaving. Just lathering up and . . ." He blew a tiny raspberry and lifted his left hand. His fingers were flaring pink.

"But you don't have any facial hair," I pointed out.

"I'm aware of the irony."

"So why were you shaving?"

"Wishful thinking." He leaned his elbow on the counter and looked wistfully at my half-eaten noodles. I quickly grabbed a few more and slipped them into my mouth before he could get any ideas.

CHAPTER 7

ONCE UPON A TIME

I managed to eat all my noodles before Viktor got his hands on them. In all fairness, he didn't try to steal any. I guess I looked pretty hungry. He probably didn't want to chance losing a finger.

By the time we were done, the streetlights were the only thing we could see through the curtains. I felt strangely tired. When I let out a yawn, Viktor slid off his stool and stood up.

"Better get this one home and tucked into bed."

"What bed?" I muttered, leaning my forearms on the cool surface in front of me. "You don't have any furniture."

"Not in the bedrooms."

"Isn't that where beds usually go?"

He shrugged and wandered over to the back door. Pulling aside the curtain, he peered out into the backyard. "We're trying to keep a low profile. Make it look like there's nothing to steal."

"You've got a ticketed front door," I pointed out. "People shouldn't be breaking in."

He turned around with a raised eyebrow. "You did."

"Yeah, well, I was stupid."

"You were hungry," Niesha said, hanging the damp dish towel on the handle of the oven to dry. She crooked her finger at me and proceeded to walk toward the darkened front of the house. I glanced at Viktor before sliding off my stool and following.

With the flick of a switch, a gorgeous living room came into view. I stopped in the doorway and gaped. Niesha paused in her rearranging of some throw pillows and looked at me with a smile.

"Surprised?"

"Why doesn't it look like a shitty drug house?"

"Because I'm not about to let my parents' place end up in that state. If they come back one day . . ."

"Nobody's coming back," I said. "It's been three years."

"Three years, two months, and fourteen days," Viktor said behind me. I edged sideways to give him room to pass. He walked over to the couch and flopped onto it, squishing the pillows Niesha had just tidied. She sighed and sat down next to him, pulling her feet up onto the cushions and sort of leaning into his side. I barely noticed the golden boy slip into the room and take a seat on a grey velvet chair.

"Is this . . . a thing?" I asked.

"We're married," Viktor said, but before I could

react to that statement, Niesha snorted and reached out to give one of his nipples a hard twist. He yelped.

"You wish. I'm way too old for you."

"The world is different now."

"It's not different enough that I'd ever marry a seventeen-year-old boy. You want me to go to jail?"

He made a dismissive sound almost like one of his raspberries. "You wouldn't go to jail."

"Being married to you would still be a pretty hefty punishment."

"How old are you?" I asked, looking around for a place to sit. The rug looked nice enough, but I didn't really want to sit on the floor. The couch had room, but sitting down there seemed like it might be weird. The tufted ottoman that served as a coffee table looked promising. As I sank down onto it, my bones almost let out a groan of relief.

"Twenty-two."

"And you're a Rifter?"

She nodded. "The oldest one I've heard of was twenty-four at the time of the Rift."

"So there's a twenty-seven-year-old Rifter out there?"

"I heard he died in that checkpoint skirmish last year."

"Kenyonville belongs to the young," Viktor said, adjusting himself so he could put his arm around Niesha's shoulders. She looked a little annoyed, but she didn't really try to move, either.

"Yeah, I noticed," I said.

"How old are you?" Niesha asked.

"Twenty."

"So you were in the school at the time."

I shook my head.

"She was playing hooky," Viktor offered.

"I was not," I snapped. "I didn't even go to that stupid school. I don't know exactly what happened."

He sat up a little straighter. "You don't know what happened?"

Niesha rolled her eyes. "Here we go."

"What? It's a good story." He pulled his arm out from behind her and stood up. Niesha reached for my hand and tugged on it. I transferred myself to the couch, which was a hell of a lot more comfortable than anything I'd plunked my butt on in years.

Viktor positioned himself in the middle of the room and planted his feet as if to steady himself. With a dramatic flourish and a mighty raspberry, he whipped up his glowing hands.

"Every time," Niesha muttered.

"In the beginning," Viktor said, his voice booming, "there was the science lab." He brought his hands forward. The glow illuminated his face with an eerie pink, highlighting the scars.

"If you mess up your other eye while you're showing off," Niesha said, "I don't want to hear any whining."

"Shh. You're ruining the mood." But he moved his

hands out to the sides, safely away from his body. "On a hump-day like any other—"

"But it wasn't like any other."

"We didn't know that at the time."

"But you know it now."

"Fine. On a very special Wednesday, some kid was working on his science project. He had some doo-dads"—he swept his right hand up dramatically—"and some thingamajigs"—the left hand did its thing—"and left all the students in awe at the powers of his mighty brain."

"That's not what I heard," Niesha said. "Wasn't everyone on their phones? Most of them missed it when it actually happened."

Viktor's glowing hands drooped a little. "Are you done?"

"Just helping you tell the story."

"You weren't even there."

"Neither were you."

He rolled his eyes. "I was in the school. Just not in the science lab. I had French that period."

Niesha leaned closer so she could whisper, "So he says. But his French is shit, so I have my doubts."

"Suddenly," Viktor boomed, either to drown out the insult or simply to continue with the story, "there was a mighty flash." He threw his right hand side-ways. Pink sparks exploded onto the wall, just below a framed family portrait.

"Knock it off!" Niesha shouted.

"It doesn't affect walls."

"My house, my rules. If you want to throw those things around, do it outside."

"Okay, okay." He shook his head, somewhat chastened. But he didn't shake the glow from his hands. "Where was I?"

"The flash," I said.

"Oh. Right. There was a mighty flash! All the kids were knocked backward off their stools. There was much screaming and gnashing of teeth."

"Which, apparently, you could hear," Niesha said.

"All the way across the school. I know a gnash when I hear one. Anyway, when they all picked themselves up off the floor, there was . . . the Rift." He stopped and stared at us expectantly. Pink tendrils still curled from his fingers, licking at his skin.

"Yeah . . . and?"

"There it was."

She snorted. "You've been telling this story for years now, and it still hasn't gotten any better."

"What do you want? A love triangle?"

"A little more description would be nice."

He shrugged and finally lowered his hands, shaking them as he did so. The pink splattered into the air as it went out. "No one got a great look. The kids were rushed out pretty quick. And nobody's been allowed back in there to look at it since."

"Would *you* go back into that school voluntarily?"

"Depends. Do I have to take a French quiz?"

She shook her head.

"I heard Permanent Marc raided the place last summer," Viktor said thoughtfully, coming to sit down on my other side. "Not sure what he would've gotten out of that."

"Food?" I asked.

He laughed. "Now I *know* you were homeschooled. Who'd want to eat old cafeteria slop?"

With a sigh, I sank back into the cushions. "You got me."

"Doesn't seem fair," Niesha said.

"What doesn't?"

"Us getting pinkhands. We weren't even there."

"It's a virus," Viktor said. "Viruses don't care about fairness."

Niesha shook her head. "Says who? Just because people can't explain things like pinkhands doesn't mean it's a virus."

"Why not? It's a Rift to who knows where. There could be a virus that came through it."

"And infected nearly everyone between the ages of ten and twenty-four, but left the rest of the population untouched? Aren't viruses supposed to spread? Why didn't my parents end up with pinkhands? Why didn't your cousin?"

"Why didn't Click?" he shot back. "He's the right age. So he's probably immune. Doesn't that suggest a virus?"

"Who's Click?" I asked. Niesha turned to me with a confused expression.

"Click." She waved her hand over at the golden boy who was sitting still and quiet in the grey chair, his legs folded up onto the seat.

"Is that a nickname?" I asked. He just smiled.

"Oh, yeah," Niesha said. "Good luck trying to pronounce his real name."

"Why do you call him Click?"

"'Cause when I first joined up with him," Viktor said, "we had to run. And he ran for, like, a whole kilometre without stopping."

Niesha let out a grunt of laughter. "Also because of his real name."

"Which is?"

"Ask him."

I turned to the boy who was still sitting there with a bemused smile on his face. "What's your name?"

He didn't say anything for a moment, and I wasn't sure if he was even going to answer. But then he opened his mouth and . . . a sound came out. It didn't really sound like a name to me. It was more like an "ah-ee" sound, followed by a click at the back of his throat. I blinked.

"See?" Viktor said. "Click."

"What language is that?"

"Heck if I know."

"Does he speak English?" I asked, realizing that Click's real name was the only word I'd ever heard the guy speak.

"He understands it. Mostly. Now."

"We think he must've been some sort of exchange student," Niesha said. "But nobody ever claimed him, and after the evacuation . . ."

"His host family just left him here?"

"Rifters weren't allowed out."

I shook my head. "But Viktor said he doesn't have pinkhands. So couldn't he have left?"

"Everyone who wanted to leave had to be tested. If they had pinkhands, they had to stay. But if his host family just left him, unable to really speak the language . . ."

"Wow. Assholes."

"He's fine," Viktor said. "Aren't you?"

Click stared at him for a moment, then gave him a thumbs up. Niesha laughed.

"I'd say so." She took a deep breath and stretched, pointing her fingers toward the ceiling. "We better get some sleep if we're going to check out that house tomorrow. I want everybody alert." Standing, she waved her hand toward the staircase just outside the living room.

"We're not going back to the cache house?" I asked.

She smirked. "You can if you want. But that basement where those two sleep is pretty rank."

"It is *not*," Viktor said with a cough of mock indignation. "How dare you?"

"How dare you only shower once a month? There's no excuse. You have running water."

"It's cold."

"Suck it up." She edged around the ottoman. "You and Click can take the master bedroom. Sleep on top of the covers, please. Or you're washing the sheets."

"Picky, picky, picky," Viktor grumbled, shooting a cheeky glance in my direction. "You don't think I smell *that* bad, do you?"

I had a feeling that much of the conversation was just good-natured ribbing. He didn't smell like much, actually, other than slightly sweaty. Who was I to talk, though? My pits hadn't seen a stick of deodorant in years.

"You *are* pretty pungent," I said, standing up. "I wasn't going to say anything, but . . ."

He gasped and threw his head back dramatically. "Scorned! I don't think I'll ever recover from this."

Niesha snorted as she took my hand and led me toward the stairs. "You better. We've got a busy day tomorrow."

CHAPTER 8

THE SLUMBER PARTY THAT WASN'T

Niesha's bedroom was a lot larger—and nicer—than my room had been. A queen-size bed took up much of the space, but there was still room for two nightstands (one of which had a charging phone lounging on its dust-free surface, a sight that was both weird and comforting in its normalcy), a tidy desk, a tall dresser, and a comfy chair positioned by the window that looked over the backyard. I stood looking out at the spangled sky, feeling awkwardly filthy. I'd showered regularly at Ayla's, but I hadn't exactly kept up on my laundry. And now that I only had one set of clothes . . .

"You can borrow some pyjamas," Niesha said, and I turned to see her enter the room, a folded towel and washcloth in hand. She set them on the dresser and pulled open a drawer near the bottom, revealing a pale rainbow of neatly folded garments. "Kittens or unicorns?"

"Huh?"

She smiled as she held up what appeared to be two oversized t-shirts, one grey with pink kittens gambolling across it, the other light green with rainbows and large-eyed unicorns scattered over the fabric.

"Has Viktor seen that one?" I asked, jutting my chin at the kitten shirt.

"Not that I know of. He hasn't seen any of my PJs. I try not to give him any fuel for his fantasies."

"Fuel?"

"He's a seventeen-year-old boy. It wouldn't take much."

"I'll take the unicorns," I said quickly, not wanting to give him any excuse to start talking about Rift kittens again if he happened to catch a glimpse.

"Good choice." She handed the t-shirt to me before expertly refolding and settling the kitten shirt back in the drawer. "Bathroom's down the hall. You can take a shower if you like."

I hesitated, gripping the unicorn shirt in both hands, fighting the urge to give my armpits a sniff. Niesha closed the drawer and straightened up as she turned to me. The expression on my face must've said *something*, because she quickly shook her head.

"You don't have to."

"I probably should."

She let out a huff of laughter. "I've gotten so used to Viktor that the stink bar is pretty high. You're nowhere near it." She paused, a little twinkle forming in her eyes. "I've got soap, though, so . . ."

Soap—any sort of body-care product—was so rare in the Zone that most of us jumped at the chance to use it when we could. I bit my lip and looked at the towel and washcloth. She reached for them and handed both to me.

"Go on. There's hot water, too. Make sure you lock the door, though."

I didn't need to be told. The last thing I wanted was a teenage boy "accidentally" stumbling into the bathroom while I happened to be naked.

Niesha must've been keeping up with the housekeeping because the bathroom was just as pristine as the rest of the house. The bathrooms in Ayla's place smelled dirty; a whiff of urine always seemed to permeate the spaces. But the bathroom I now stood in smelled clean and fresh. There were no yellowish splashes on the wall around the toilet. The whole room looked almost sterile, decorated in shades of silver and white. After double-checking the lock on the door, I stripped down and laid the garments on the closed lid of the toilet. My t-shirt and jeans were the only clothes I had left, and they weren't looking so great. The jeans were filthy and ragged around the bottom hems. The t-shirt had once been a pristine white, but the yellow areas under the arms seemed to get bigger with each passing day. Even washing it—when I had been able to wash it—hadn't done much about that.

There was, in fact, a bar of off-white soap sitting in a soap dish in the shower. I smiled as I turned on the water. The steamy streams pounded against the bottom of the tub, forming a comforting cocoon of noise, especially when I stepped in and pulled the silvery shower curtain closed. I stood there for a few moments, watching the water cascade off my body, almost surprised that I couldn't see dirt pouring down the drain. I supposed our little apocalypse wasn't really the sort that left people mud-caked and existing in various shades of brown. Ours was just . . . sweaty.

—

When I stepped out of the bathroom in the unicorn shirt, I was relieved to find the hallway empty. The door to the master bedroom was closed, and I couldn't hear anything from the other side. I tiptoed quickly back to Niesha's room, holding my folded jeans, t-shirt, and jacket against my chest. When I got there, she leaped up from the chair by the window and hurried to close the door behind me. Then she took my clothes and placed them on top of the dresser.

"Nobody disturbed you?" she asked, tilting her head toward the large bed where the covers were already turned down.

"No. Should I have been expecting a disturbance?"

She smiled as she slipped under the covers. "I wouldn't have been surprised."

I walked over to the bed and sat down on the edge. Even from that, I could tell it was a really nice mattress. And the covers were just as plush. I'd always had a quilt, but Niesha had a duvet that I suspected was stuffed with marshmallow fluff, judging by its feel. A long sigh escaped before I could stop it.

"When's the last time you slept in a proper bed?" she asked as she arranged the covers around her body.

"It's been a while."

"Where have you been living?"

I got into the bed and pulled my body under the duvet, which was super distracting because it felt like I'd just burrowed into a cloud. "I like your bed."

"So do I." Propping herself up on one elbow, she raised her eyebrows as she stared at me. I bit my lip. "It's fine. I get it if you don't want to talk. It's hard to know who to trust in this town these days."

"It's not that."

"Isn't it?"

I shrugged, but my mind whirled, trying to figure out how much it would be safe to say. It wasn't like I would be going back to Ayla's. For one thing, it had those two awful little girls who'd stolen my stuff. My uncomfortable pillow and ugly blanket might've already been pilfered, too. So what was left to go back to? I could sleep on a hard floor just about anywhere.

"It was just some townhouse with a bunch of other

Rifters," I said at last. "I slept on the living room floor."

"No furniture?"

"Not that I saw. I guess they'd cleared it out to make more room."

She shook her head. "I've heard about those places. Makes me glad I was a legal adult when the Rift happened."

"Some kids seemed to want a never-ending slumber party."

"Bet that got old fast."

I shrugged, staring up at the ceiling. "I wasn't there for very long."

She didn't ask where I'd been before Ayla's. Instead, she sighed and flopped back onto her pillow. Her hair, loose from its ponytail, spread out like a black cloud. "Sometimes it seems like things change all the time in Kenyonville. And other times, they don't change at all. People come and go."

"Yeah."

"I'm not saying you have to leave. Hell, it's nice to have some female company for a change."

"Are Viktor and Click over here a lot?"

"More than most of the others. I think Viktor gets bored easily."

"Little kids do."

She snorted. "He's smarter than he seems. And he's been a good asset. They both have. Sure, they're here all the time, eating my food and stinking up the place, but they also don't complain. Okay . . . Viktor complains, but he eventually does what needs to be done. Can't ask for much more than that."

"How long have they been working for you?"

She twisted her brow as if she were trying to do the math. "Two years? No, it was more than that. They were here for that first winter. That's when Viktor really started digging in his heels about showering."

"Why?"

"That cache house has a gas water heater."

"And there's no gas?" I guessed.

"Yeah. This house is all electric, so hot water has never been an issue."

I thought back to Grandpa's house. Our warmth had come from baseboard heaters. I'd never really thought about the hot water tank . . . but there had been hot water up until the day I'd left, so it must've been electric, too.

"I actually caught them sneaking into the distribution cache," Niesha said, drawing my attention back to her.

"Seriously?"

"Yeah. A couple of us were getting stuff organized for handing out the next day, and there was this huge thump near the front of the house. I went to check it out and found Viktor on the floor just inside the window. I could see Click standing outside, staring in. And Viktor just stands up, makes his little fart noises, and says—"

"Stick 'em up!"

The voice coming through the closed bedroom door made Niesha jump. But then she let out a groan as she pulled the duvet up over her head. "Seriously?"

"You better be telling the story properly, Niesh."

"Isn't it past your bedtime?"

"Nah. I'm a big boy. I can stay up a little later now." The door squeaked open, revealing a grinning, half-dressed Viktor. Niesha threw off the duvet and sat up, glaring.

"Go to bed."

"Why don't I ever get invited to the special slumber parties?"

"Oh, my god, Viktor. That's not even a thing."

"Looks like a thing." He raised his eyebrows, then snuck a cheeky wink at me with his cloudy eye. I sat up slowly, keeping the duvet tight around my body. It wasn't like the unicorn shirt was see-through or anything, but I was painfully aware that I didn't have anything on my bottom half other than a pair of worn panties.

"Léa will still be here in the morning. You can annoy her then."

He placed a hand on his chest, his faux offence apparent. "I," he said, "am not annoying."

"No? Then what are you?"

"Hmm. Good question." He took a casual step into the room, his black socks silent on the carpet. He'd taken off his jacket and jeans and was wearing nothing but a black t-shirt, navy boxers, and socks.

"Nice outfit," Niesha said.

"My jeans are kind of dirty and your parents' bed is kind of white. Didn't want you to make me do laundry in the morning."

"I told you, sleep—"

"—on top. Yeah, we are."

Niesha pointed her finger out the door. "Go."

"Why do *you* get to have Léa all to yourself?"

"I don't know what you think we're doing in here, but—"

"Well . . ."

"Jesus," she said, holding up a hand to cut him off. "Forget I said anything."

"Done." Before I knew what was happening, he'd taken a few running steps and launched himself toward the bed. I squeaked and pulled my legs up so he wouldn't land on them.

"Viktor! What the hell?"

He landed on his front, sort of draped across the end of the bed. "What? You said to forget—"

"—that I told you to get out." She let out a long-suffering sigh. "I *was* just telling Léa that you weren't that bad, but now . . ."

"Aw."

"If you don't go back to your room right now, you're going back to the cache house."

He rolled onto his side to give her a look of disbelief. "Come on!"

"Click's your roommate, not me."

"Click's all tucked in and fast asleep."

"So why aren't you?"

"I'm not sleepy. And I have no one to talk to."

"Will you *please* go to bed?"

He turned to me. "You can sleep with me and Click if you want. The bed in there is *huge.*"

"She doesn't want to sleep with your smelly ass," Niesha said.

"Yeah, but *I'm* not going to force her to go to sleep at nine o'clock like a grandma."

"So what's the plan? Stay up until midnight? You get argumentative when you don't get enough sleep."

"I do not."

She just grunted. Viktor sat up, tightened his ponytail with a sniff, and scooted off the bed.

"Fine. Then I shall bid you goodnight." He stood, gave us a little bow, and swivelled on his heel before walking out into the hallway.

"Close the door!"

He must've heard her words, but he ignored them. I looked at Niesha, who shook her head.

"Better get used to it," she said, keeping her voice low so he wouldn't hear. She didn't get up to close the door, though, and she didn't ask me to do it. She just snuggled back down under the duvet. I didn't really mind. I was used to open doors. In fact, I preferred them.

There was less chance of nasty surprises that way.

CHAPTER 9

THE HOUSE ON MONROE STREET

The sky seemed a lot bluer. The air smelled a lot sweeter. And my body felt stronger than it had in ages.

I wasn't sure if it was a good night's rest in a soft bed (I'd fallen asleep shortly after Viktor's departure), the breakfast of an oatmeal cookie and a glass of water (I still wasn't allowed to eat much . . . but, damn, that cookie was good), or the company (I hadn't spent much time with other people in months), but everything just felt . . . better. As we wended our way through side streets and laneways toward the house at Havilland and Monroe, Viktor kept up a lively chatter that Niesha kept shooting down with exasperated barbs that never seemed to have much effect. Click and I remained silent, though it didn't really feel awkward not to talk.

"I'll go first," Niesha said as we trudged down the

sidewalk on Monroe Street, approaching our destination. Usually, Lex would've heard someone coming and started barking. But the still morning remained quiet, punctuated only by a few chirps of birds and the distant sound of what sounded like an electric lawnmower. "That reminds me," she said.

"What reminds you?" Viktor asked absently. He was staring up at the houses as we passed them. In that part of town, they were older, some of them three-storey buildings with creaky porches and lots of peeling paint.

"The lawn needs mowing."

"On whose place?"

"Both, probably."

"I'd have to haul the dang mower all the way over from your house."

"So?"

"So, do you want it stolen?"

"I thought you struck terror into the hearts of potential muggers."

He snorted. "Only in the dark. In the sunlight, it's pretty clear I'm just a guy with a scar, not a dangerously mangled mutant." He started to drag one foot, leaning sideways until he stumbled into Niesha with a slurpy-sounding growl. She shoved him away with both hands.

"Just mow the lawn, smartass."

"Why can't you do it?"

"Do you want cookies?"

"Not raisin ones," he muttered. "But, point taken." He shuffled to a stop and peered up at the house beside us. "This it?"

I nodded and looked up the steps into the shadowy porch. The door was still closed, the way I'd left it, the ticket hanging limp from its nail.

"Looks occupied to me," he said. Niesha turned to me, a quizzical expression on her face.

"There's nobody here," I said quickly. "There used to be a dog. Lex. But he'd be barking his head off if he were still here."

"Maybe the dog ran away," Viktor said.

"Then why was the door open?"

"Maybe that's *how* the dog ran away."

"Nobody answered when I called." I let out a long sigh. "Look, if you don't want to go in there, fine. I'll do it myself. Maybe Joshua will want whatever's in there."

"Whoa," Niesha said, holding up one hand. "Why bring Joshua into it?"

"Because I . . . I have to do jobs for *someone.*"

The look she was giving me was equal parts confusion, hurt, and disappointment. I looked down at my shoes.

"Why would you want to work for that donkey-butt?" Viktor asked. I raised my gaze to glare at him.

"He pays. If the haul is good enough."

"And you think I don't pay?" Niesha asked.

I shrugged. She must've thought I was an ungrateful

bitch, eating her food, using her shower, sleeping in her bed. And there I was, talking about giving the spoils of this venture to Joshua, the greedy little pissant who was her competition.

She sighed. "You don't owe me anything. If you really want to work for Joshua, that's up to you."

"But—" Viktor began, only to stop when Niesha shook her head.

"What do you really want, Léa?"

The question seemed like a trap. I took a deep breath. "Food," I said slowly.

"No. What do you *want?*"

For some reason, my throat got tight. And I panicked. I hadn't cried in years. Showing any sign of weakness wasn't very bright. I hadn't even cried when I'd lost my toe, and that whole episode had hurt like hell.

"Nothing," I said after swallowing the tight lump in my throat.

"Everyone wants something," Viktor said.

"Yeah, well, maybe I just want you to shut up. If you don't want to go in there, fine. Then go home, mow your lawn, pick the raisins out of your cookies, and let me get on with it. Okay?"

He cast a look at Niesha, eyebrow raised. I couldn't quite read it. He might've been amused or insulted. Knowing him, though, he was probably just trying to think up some comeback he thought was funny.

"We're already here," Niesha said at last. "Might as

well check it out. But we're knocking first. If someone answers, we're not going in. Agreed?"

"Fine by me," Viktor said, even though Niesha seemed to be directing her words at me more than anyone else. I nodded meekly and remained behind with the guys while she slowly made her way up the porch steps. They creaked a little under her weight but seemed solid enough. "Holler if you need help," Viktor added.

She shot an annoyed look at him over her shoulder. He held up his hands.

"What? You might. You don't know what's in there."

"Probably nothing," she said, keeping her voice low, "if it's been abandoned."

"And if it hasn't," he mused, "what's in there will be worse than nothing."

I looked up at him standing beside me. From that angle, all I could see was the scar. "Worse?"

He turned to me so I could fully see his frown. "Don't tell me you haven't come across any stinkers in the last three years."

"What's a stinker?"

"Body." He shook his head and turned back to Niesha, who had just knocked on the door and was standing on her toes to try to peer through the shallow window embedded within it.

"Don't call them that."

"What else do I call them?"

"I don't know. But not that. It's . . . disrespectful."

He opened his mouth to say something else, then seemed to think better of it. Instead, he angled his chin toward the house. "Hear anything?" he called.

"No. And the doorbell's not working."

"You going to go in?"

She turned and gave him an annoyed look. "You going to stop rushing me? If there *is* somebody in there, you better get ready to run because I don't feel like nursing any burns today."

"Aw. And here I was, itching for a good pinkball fight."

"Would you stop calling them that, please?"

"What? Why?" he asked, though the way his mouth was twitching, he knew the answer perfectly well. Niesha ignored him and braced her hand on the door handle. The latch clunked as she pressed down, and the door swung open into the space. She leaned inside and sniffed, holding up her hand as if she wanted us to keep quiet. After a few moments, she waved that hand, beckoning us toward the porch.

"I don't hear anything," she said when we were all gathered around the door. "But that doesn't mean shit. So let's just do a quick sweep. If things go sideways, we meet at the park on the next block. Okay?"

"Sideways . . . how?" I asked. She shook her head.

"If someone's in there. Or if the someone who isn't there right now happens to come home. Just be prepared for every possibility." She started to slip off her shoes, then seemed to think better of it.

"Bad idea," Viktor said.

"Yeah, I know. Force of habit. Keep your shoes on. But be respectful. This could still be somebody's house." She took a tiptoeing step inside, gripping the straps of the backpack on her shoulders. "Viktor, you and Léa look upstairs. Click and I will do a sweep down here."

"What about the third floor?" Viktor asked. "We have to do that, too?"

"Oh, gee. Another few square feet in addition to some bedrooms." She rolled her eyes. "Do you really want to switch? The floor with the kitchen's going to be a lot more work."

"You'll probably find more stuff."

She sighed. "Are you going to give me a hard time all day?"

"Are you going to let me?"

With a grunt, she gave his shoulder a shove. He stumbled into the bannister. "Go. And don't talk Léa's ear off. I want to get this done before next week."

He snorted and leaped for the stairs, taking them two at a time. Niesha glanced at me apologetically. I pretended like I didn't care that I'd just gotten saddled with the most annoying partner ever and reached for the railing. My legs still felt weaker than they should have, so it was nice to have the support as I made my way up to the second floor. When I got to the top, I found myself in a cramped sort of hallway, similar to the one in Grandpa's house. Five doors led off the landing; all but one were closed. The open door swung into the hallway, making a nuisance of itself in the already-cramped space. Viktor was leaning against the frame, peering into the shadows beyond.

"What's in there?" I asked, stepping closer. "What's *up* there?" I corrected myself.

"No idea. Can't see much." He reached inside the space, fumbling at the wall as if searching for a light switch.

"I'm not going up there if there's no light."

He snorted and turned to me. "You've got light wherever you go."

"I'm not using pinkhands as a flashlight. That's how people accidentally melt their faces."

"Excuse me. It was a shaving accident, not a lighting accident. Remember?"

"Do you really think you should be waving those things around at all?"

He grasped the edge of the door and pushed it closed. The hallway suddenly seemed both more and less cramped. "If the situation calls for it, I do what I must." Regarding the other four doors, he frowned. "Shall we do this together or separately?"

"Separately," I said quickly.

"You sure?"

"Yes," I snapped. "I don't need your help."

"Okay . . . but if there's a stinker in the room you pick, don't come crying to me."

Now that he mentioned it, the house did smell a little

funky. But there were all sorts of reasons why that might be the case. Someone not keeping on top of throwing out rotting food in the fridge was the most likely explanation. I'd had personal experience with that.

"If I find any bodies," I said, "I'll be sure to let you know."

"I'm sure I'll be able to smell it if you do."

"Yeah? How will you know you're not just smelling yourself?"

He laughed and gave my shoulder a gentle shove. "Nice one." He reached back for a moment to tighten his ponytail, almost as if he were trying to salvage his dignity. Then he reached for the nearest doorknob. I stepped toward the front of the house, heading for the door at the end of the cramped space. I could hear Niesha and Click rummaging around downstairs, and the sound was strangely comforting. We were obviously the only living things in that house (unless there were some critters in the attic), and I felt the tension in my shoulders that I'd been carrying all morning start to ease a little.

But that tension came roaring right back, causing my whole body to lock up, when I opened that door. The stench hit me so hard that I almost passed out. My hands flared in a stinging explosion of colour as I stumbled backward with a scream.

CHAPTER 10

BAD DOG

Viktor was shouting. At me. I didn't realize why until a moment later when he grabbed me by the face. My scream cut off into a hiccup.

"It's okay," he said, his voice pitched like he was talking to a wild animal. "It's okay. You're all right."

I stared into his mismatched eyes for a moment as his words tried to land. Nothing seemed to be making any sense. All I could see, as if layered over his face like a horrible movie projection, was that scene. I closed my eyes with a shudder. The next thing I knew, Viktor's arms were around me. I went rigid, but I didn't pull away.

"What the hell's going on up there?" Niesha shouted, and I heard thundering footsteps on the staircase.

"Nothing much," Viktor said. "Just what we expected."

"Damn it." She retched. "Close that door."

I pushed away from Viktor, who let go quickly, leaving his arms sort of hanging in the air. "You can't," I said, my voice trembling like I was sitting on an off-balance washing machine.

"Of course we can," she said, reaching past me for the knob. But, as she peered into the room, she stopped. "Holy shit," she breathed. And then, "God fucking damn it."

Viktor cleared his throat. "Are you done?"

She turned to him in disbelief. "And what was *your* reaction to that?"

"To what?" He frowned and stepped closer to peer over her shoulder. "Oh."

His reaction seemed so inadequate that I started to laugh. But it was a wheezy sound, and it didn't sound right at all. I bent over and placed my hands on my knees as the rusty giggles poured out of me.

"Relax," Viktor said.

Niesha coughed. "Are you seeing what I'm seeing?"

"Not you. Léa."

"I am relaxed," I wheezed, standing back up. "Perfectly relaxed. Isn't this great? Aren't you having fun? I am. Yeah. I can't wait to dream about this and replay it over and over in my—" I broke off as Click edged past me, into the room. "Don't!" I shouted. "He'll—" I clamped my mouth shut as he held up his hand. The three of us watched as he walked through the room, over the body that was sprawled beside the bed, as if it had fallen out . . . or been dragged out. A low growl curled through the air as he knelt down beside the bed and bent low to peer under it.

"Click," Niesha said, "be careful."

"If that thing eats your face, too . . ." Viktor said. That was all it took. I stumbled away from them, searching for an appropriate spot. But when I realized there wasn't one, I just let it go. The remains of my meagre breakfast splattered onto the carpet.

"Jesus," Niesha muttered. "Okay. Everybody out. This isn't worth it."

"What if there's something great behind one of the other doors?" Viktor asked.

"I don't care if there's a full fucking vending machine behind one of those doors." She grabbed his elbow and steered him back toward the stairs. "Click! Leave it."

But the growling didn't stop. I dragged the back of my wrist over my mouth. For some reason, all I could taste was raisins. I turned around to find Click standing in the doorway, holding a scruffy white bundle in his arms. Lex was shaking, and his front paws seemed to be clinging to the guy's arm like those of a scared little kid. Niesha shook her head.

"No. No way."

"Why not?" Viktor asked. She just gaped at him.

"Are you serious? The last thing you need is a dog. Especially a face-eating dog."

"He's vicious," I said. My throat burned as I spoke.

"Doesn't look vicious," Viktor said. "Did he bite you or something?"

"He ate his owner's face."

"Haven't you ever been that hungry?"

"What's the matter with you?"

Niesha sighed. "Viktor gets inappropriately stupid in stressful situations. Ignore him." She turned back to Click. "Leave the dog here."

But Click's arms tightened. So, it seemed, did Lex's. With a grunt of frustration, Niesha reached past Click for the doorknob. He skittered out of the way as she pulled the door closed. The stench still hung heavy in the tiny space, though, embellished with my own vomit.

"This isn't over," she said. "You better believe there's going to be a discussion about this."

"If we want to keep a dog in our house—" Viktor began.

"First of all, it's not *your* house. It's one of my caches. You work for me, remember?"

"Somebody's on a power trip."

"Are you serious? Grow up, Viktor. And use your brain. What the hell are you going to feed that thing? It can't survive on Cheeznudles, and there's barely enough real food to go around as it is."

"So what's your solution? Leave him here at the buffet?"

"That's disgusting. And beside the point. What are you going to do with him when you go out on jobs?

You can't take him with you," she said quickly when he opened his mouth to speak. "You know what that is?" She pointed at Lex. "That's leverage. A potential ransom situation. You start loving something like that, some vulnerable thing a shit-faced boss could take away from you just to make a point, and you've lost the upper hand."

"You let me keep Click."

"Click's not a dog. And he can take care of himself. He's managed to survive without pinkhands, even saddled with a reckless moron like you."

"I'll give you the moron part, but I'm not reckless."

"Says the guy who's arguing to keep a dog in post-Rift Kenyonville."

He threw up his hands. "Then what do you suggest? Leave him here? Turn him loose?" He looked over at Click, whose fingers were gently massaging the dog's ear. Lex seemed to be relaxing a little. "At this point, he's probably going to follow us home. And I'm not willing to be mean to him to scare him away."

Niesha looked pissed. She glared at the dog. Then she glared at Viktor.

"Do you want to be mean to a dog?" he asked.

"Do you want to end up like his owner?"

He snorted. "Unlikely."

"You don't know that."

"The guy's hair was white. He wasn't young. For all we know, he died of natural causes."

"Getting mauled by a dog isn't natural."

"You think that little hairball could kill a man?"

She looked at Lex. He looked right back at her, still trembling, as if he somehow knew his future was at stake.

"He was probably desperate," Viktor said. "The door was closed. Who knows how long he'd been stuck in there?"

"Why was the front door open?" I asked. They all turned to me. I swallowed hard, still tasting stomach acid. "When I first came here, the door was open. If the guy died in the bedroom . . ."

"He couldn't have opened the front door," Niesha finished for me. "So somebody else did. Shit."

"Has this place already been searched?" Viktor asked.

"I don't know. But there's a bunch of stuff in the kitchen, so if it *has* been searched . . ."

"Somebody's coming back for the stuff."

Niesha shook her head. "Right. And we don't know when, but we should assume it's soon. So—" She broke off. Viktor opened his mouth to say something, but she reached up and clamped her hand over it. I just stood there, heart pounding. That was all I could hear for a moment. But then I heard something else.

Lex let out a whine as his head snapped toward the sound of voices drifting up the stairs.

CHAPTER 11

DEPTH PERCEPTION

We all sort of froze. Niesha was the first to break free, waving her hand toward one of the doors. Viktor didn't waste any time; he pushed it open and grabbed my hand. Out of the corner of my eye, I saw Niesha and Click disappear into one of the other rooms. Viktor closed the door, careful not to let it make too much noise.

The room we found ourselves in was a bathroom. It was kind of dark, despite the window; it must've been on the north side of the house, at an angle from the morning sunshine. Besides a grotty old clawfoot tub with a mildewed curtain, there was a toilet, a sink, some sort of spindle with a single roll of toilet paper skewered on it, and another door. I pulled my sweaty hand out of Viktor's and hurried to the window. Unfortunately, it was on the side of the house . . . and, on that particular house, that meant a pretty steep drop to the ground below, since there was no first-floor roof to land on.

I turned around to see Viktor grasping the doorknob on the other door. But he wasn't opening it.

"Hurry up," I whispered. He waved his hand at me in a gesture that clearly said he wanted me to be quiet. I tiptoed closer so I could whisper into his ear. He leaned down a little to accommodate me. "What are you waiting for?"

"We don't know what's on the other side."

"Well, we know what's downstairs, and unless you want to meet them . . ."

"We've already found one body. What if there are more?"

"I think the guy lived alone."

He sighed and turned the knob. I braced myself, both for the potential scene as well as the potential smell, but when he pulled open the door—carefully, to try to still the creak in the hinges—we were met with nothing but a slightly musty scent. The room didn't have a bed, but it was full. Stuffed bookcases lined the walls. Cardboard boxes were stacked in piles almost as tall as me. As we stepped into the room, Viktor peeked into an open one, which was too high for me to see.

"More books," he whispered. He stepped closer to the window, only to catch his toe on one of the boxes. The thump as he tried to steady himself echoed through the room. We both froze, listening.

I felt like I might be sick again, even though there

was nothing left in my stomach. All I wanted to do was get out of that house. A bit of food wasn't worth what I'd had to experience that morning. At that point, even a gourmet meal at Kenyonville's finest bistro wouldn't have been enough to compensate.

The voices downstairs continued steadily, and I wondered if they'd even heard Viktor's misstep. They didn't seem to be coming closer, at any rate. If they weren't in the kitchen, they wouldn't have been directly under us. They might not have heard anything.

Viktor watched the floor carefully for obstacles as he picked his way toward the window, stepping over piles of yellowed newspapers and a stack of folded blankets that appeared to be covered in pet hair. (Since the hair was black—and Lex was white—I assumed it was from some other pet that was long gone.) When he reached the window, he stared out for only a moment before reaching for the latch.

"What are you doing?" I whispered, hurrying forward to grab his arm. "They'll hear that when you open it."

"You want to be stuck in here when they check these rooms?"

"They might not come upstairs."

"If they're thorough, they will." He shook me off and turned back to the window. It was an old one, the wooden frame covered in peeling white paint. He grabbed the lip on the bottom edge and slowly worked it upward. It didn't make as much noise as I'd thought it might, but I was still extremely aware of every sound we were making. When the window was open, he nudged me toward it.

I didn't want to go first, but I didn't really want to be the only person left standing in that room if the door burst open, either. I got one leg over the sill, then curled my body low to fit through the opening. There was a piece of roof right outside, a little too steep for my taste, but not so bad that I couldn't get traction with the sole of my shoe. I held the edge of the window tightly as I pulled my other leg out and crawled across the shingles, getting out of the way so Viktor could climb outside, too. I pressed my back against the side of the house, leery of the drop. The first floor wasn't actually at ground level, which meant the stupid house probably had some sort of basement. It also meant that a fall from our position would be more than one storey.

"Spit," Viktor said when he'd wrangled his long limbs out the window. He crouched in front of it, staring at me with a concerned expression. "You okay?"

"Spit?"

He shook his head. "You and Niesha say something else." He reached out to close the window.

"Don't. They'll hear you."

"Yeah, and if they see an open window in an otherwise shut-tight house, they're going to take a peek out here."

I put my head in my hands. Out of the corner of my eye, I saw him struggle with the window. A moment later, he joined me, pressing his back against the wall as his boots scuffed on the shingles.

"We should've stayed together," he muttered.

"Why?" I asked, letting go of my head. "So they can get four for the price of two?"

"There's safety in numbers."

"Click's holding a dog. And you said he doesn't have pinkhands."

"He doesn't."

"So we wouldn't be much better off. We'd be worse off. At least now, *some* of us might make it out of here alive."

He snorted. "You think scavengers are that ruthless?" As if a thought had just occurred to him, he turned toward me, soles slipping a little on the roof. "Dang, Léa. What happened to you out there?"

"Nothing," I snapped, maybe a little too loudly. I took a deep breath and let it out as slowly as I could. "I'm fine. Look at me."

"Yeah, I'm looking. You look terrified."

"Shut up, will you?"

"Just trying to help."

"If you really want to help, you'll figure out how we're going to get out of this mess. You brought us out here, so . . ."

"We can wait."

"For how long? And how will we know if they've left? What if they're setting up a new cache house? Then we're stuck up here."

"We're not stuck." He leaned forward, peering past me. Before I could stop him, he'd gotten up onto his feet in a low crouch and started crab-walking toward the side of the house.

"If you fall, I'm not—"

"You don't have to hold my hand and kiss my boo-boos."

"I was going to say, 'I'm not going to cry at your funeral.'"

"You'd actually have a funeral for me? I'm touched." He leaned forward on his hands and knees and peered around the corner. "But it looks like you won't have to."

"What? Why?"

"Come look."

I really didn't want to move. But staying on a sloping piece of roof covered in rotting shingles didn't seem like something I could sustain in the long term, either. So, keeping my shoulder against the wall beside me, I crawled over to where he knelt. As soon as I saw what he was looking at, my heart sank.

"You better not be suggesting what I think you're suggesting," I said.

"What? It's not that far."

"I'm not jumping from the roof of a house onto the roof of a garage."

"Why not?"

"For one thing, that garage looks like it's about to fall over. The first one who tries it is probably going to go straight through the roof."

"It's not *that* bad."

"Are you a structural engineer?"

"Are you?"

"Shut up. Second, I think you're overestimating my abilities. And the length of my legs. I can't jump ten feet, even with a running start."

He snorted. "That's not ten feet. It's maybe five. Tops."

"Says the guy who's blind in one eye. I'm not staking my life on your depth perception."

"First of all, that eye is not completely blind. It can see light and shadows and some colours."

"I don't think that's going to help in this situation."

He sat back on his heels with a sigh. "Do you have any other suggestions?"

"No."

"Then unless you want to stay up here and become a really macabre roof ornament . . ."

I gaped at him. "I thought you said we could wait!"

"And you said you didn't want to get stuck up here."

"You don't have to listen to me."

"Why wouldn't I? We're partners now, aren't we? It's in both of our best interests to listen to each other." He started crawling around the corner.

"Viktor!" I whispered, my voice getting lost beneath the shuffle of his knees and toes on the shingles. "Fuck."

"I know I said I'd listen to you," he said, glancing

back over his shoulder, "but do I have to listen to that?"

"Yes, you fucking do."

He chuckled and turned around to keep crawling. Within a few seconds, he was in line with the garage. It was a good thing, too, because that piece of roof ended as it ran up against a jutting-out piece of wall. Probably the stairwell on the inside. Luckily, there were no windows around there, so nobody could see what we were about to do. Or try to do. I was pretty sure this was a terrible idea, but Viktor seemed set on it. To be honest, I didn't really see any other options myself . . . so I followed him.

"Be careful," I whispered as he stood up and pressed his back against the wall, staring determinedly across at the garage roof. It definitely looked more like ten feet to me, but thanks to the piece of roof on which we were cowering, we were at least going to get a bit of a running start. And the garage was lower, too. Maybe we *could* do this.

"If I don't make it," he said, his voice taking on a morose tone, "I want my gold watch to go to Niesha. Click gets the beach house."

"And what do I get?"

He turned to me with a wicked grin. "You," he said, "get the honour of witnessing my tragic death. Tell people I was a hero."

"And what if I die a few seconds later?"

With a snort, he turned back to the garage and his

impending jump. "You better not be stupid enough to try it right after watching me die." Before I could think of a retort, he pounded down the roof and launched himself into the air.

I sucked in a gasp. I wasn't sure if he'd just wanted to be extra sure he didn't come up short, or if he really did have shitty depth perception. But the jump took him almost to the middle point of the garage roof. Momentum took him over the top. He twisted hard, coming down on his knees to try to stop himself. But it wasn't enough. He disappeared over the far side a moment later, a startled expression on his face.

"Viktor!" My shout was way too loud. I knew it as soon as the word was out of my mouth, but my panic wouldn't allow me to modulate my volume. I waited, hoping to hear his voice. "Fuck!" I whispered, casting around for something that would help. *What the hell are you looking for, moron? You're on an empty roof.* Jumping had just gone to the very bottom of my list of things I wanted to do. I looked back at the corner of the house. *Maybe, if I'm quiet, I can make it back inside. Niesha and Click might need help, anyway, and I can't help them if I'm waffling out here on the roof.*

But before I could even make a move to turn around, something caught my eye. I sucked in a breath . . . just as Viktor staggered from around the side of the garage.

"Are you okay?" I whispered as loudly as I dared. He peered up at me as he walked closer.

"Fine. Just don't overshoot. It's a mess back there."

"A mess of what?"

"Bushes. I don't know. I'm not a botanist." He tilted his head to look up at the gap. "That's not five feet."

"No shit. So why'd you hurl yourself over the other side?"

"Too much adrenaline, I guess." He waved his hand. "Your turn."

"After seeing that?"

"What? I'm not dead."

"You could've been if you'd impaled yourself when you fell off the garage."

He snorted, but he didn't say anything. He just waved his hand again.

"I can't."

"Yes, you can. Look . . . I'll catch you if you fall."

"How?" I snapped. "You don't know if I'll go too far or not far enough. You can't be in two places at once."

"So just aim for the middle. You've got two good eyes. I'm sure you can do it."

He might've been sure, but I wasn't. My legs shaking, I stood up and pressed myself back against the wall. *It's ten feet,* I told myself. *If that. If he can do it with only one good eye, it'll be a piece of cake for you.*

I closed my eyes for a moment. When I opened them again, I braced my hands against the wall behind me. Viktor gave me an encouraging nod. And I ran.

It all would've been fine if my foot hadn't slipped. It

was the foot that was supposed to launch me across the gap, of course. I knew I wasn't going to make it, even as I flailed through the air. Viktor said something that sounded like a curse but probably wasn't, and then I hit the garage roof, stomach first.

"Hold on!" he shouted, but my fingers were no match for the weight of my lower body, which hadn't even made it onto the roof. I slid down, pulling up my shirt in the process, and I felt the rough shingles graze my skin. A moment later, I was falling through the air again . . . but not for long. As my feet hit the hard ground, I felt a snap, and I crumpled into a heap.

The pain didn't hit me at first. I was just glad to be alive. Viktor rushed over, trying to help me sit up.

"What happened? Are you okay?"

"No, I'm not okay," I snapped. My eyes watered as the pain started to seep into my consciousness. I fixed him with a hot glare and shoved him away. "I *told* you I wouldn't make it."

"But you did."

"I fucking broke something, you asshole! How the hell am I supposed to walk with—"

I broke off as a shower of pink ricocheted off the side of the garage, splattering on my legs. I let out a squeal of surprise as my hands flared. Viktor didn't even stop to see who was lobbing Riftballs at us. He scooped me up into his arms and took off down the gap between the garage and the house, heading for the street. I tried to hold on to him with my forearms, keeping my uncontrolled pinkhands away from his body. Over his shoulder, I saw the two figures coming after us.

"Shit!" I shouted, realizing a moment later that my mouth was right next to Viktor's ear.

"What?"

"Run!"

He did, somehow, even though he was carrying me. I saw one of our pursuers raise his hands. Before I could think, I drew my right arm back like I was about to throw a baseball. The two guys stopped. But I didn't. I hurled the ball of pink energy toward them. They dove out of the way, letting it splatter harmlessly on the garage door.

"What are you doing?" Viktor asked, panting. "Are you throwing pinkballs?"

I shook the energy from my hands, sending sparks flying, and grabbed his shoulders to steady myself. "Just run. Go!"

CHAPTER 12

IS THERE A DOCTOR IN THE HOUSE?

Viktor kept running while I kept looking back over his shoulder. But as we headed down Havilland, the view of the house was eventually obscured by overgrown shrubbery. I couldn't hear anything, either. No angry shouts. No pounding footsteps.

"They're not following us," I said at last.

"Good." He slowed to a walk.

"You can put me down now."

"I thought you broke something."

"You can't carry me."

He grunted in amusement. "Isn't that what I'm doing?"

I leaned back a little so I could focus on his face. "You're not *that* strong. If you drop me . . ."

"I'm not going to drop you. I think I can manage. You don't weigh that much."

"Put me down," I said, trying to pull my legs out of his grip.

"Do you *want* me to drop you?"

"I want you to let go of me."

"And then what? You going to hop all the way to the park?"

"It's not that far."

"And then all the way home?"

"Who said I was going home with you?"

"It's closer than Niesha's house."

"Yeah, and it's inhabited by a couple of guys who don't bathe regularly."

"Click bathes."

"Click's not the problem."

He smiled and hitched me up in his arms. Resigning myself to being carried—for the moment—I sighed and looked ahead of us down the sidewalk.

"Where are you going?"

"The park."

"And you're taking the scenic route?"

"Do you want to go back to that corner and take Monroe? 'Cause I don't."

I turned to look back the way we'd come. "Do you think Niesha and Click made it out?"

"Niesha's smart. And Click is . . ."

"What?" I asked, turning back to him. He shook his head a little.

"Smart. But in a different way. He sees things the

rest of us don't. Comes up with solutions we wouldn't have thought of."

"Well, we can't all be reckless morons who throw ourselves off roofs."

"Technically, that was a transfer from one roof to another."

"Until you fell off the far side."

He laughed. "Are you mocking my dismount?"

"Yeah. One out of ten for style."

He let out another grunt of laughter but didn't say anything else. I fell silent, too, and let him concentrate on walking.

—

Niesha and Click were already at the park by the time Viktor sort of staggered onto the grassy expanse. I could feel his arms shaking, but he didn't let on that he was struggling. As we made our way over to where the others were sitting on the grass, Niesha looked up, shielding her eyes from the sun.

"What happened?"

"Long story," Viktor said, finally releasing my legs so he could place me gently on the grass. As soon as my left foot touched the ground, a spike of pain zinged up my leg. I grunted and pulled it up, then sat awkwardly.

"*Stupid* story," I muttered. "It's a wonder this guy is even still alive."

Niesha sighed. "Why? What'd he do? Make you jump out the window?"

"Close."

"We *climbed* out the window," he said, folding his long legs so he could sit down beside me. I edged away, only to suck in a gasp as my ankle jostled. Click, who was sitting a few feet away, looked at me, his golden eyes shadowed by a heavy frown. Lex was sitting beside him, panting; it wasn't that hot out, so it was probably from stress. I couldn't really blame him.

"Yeah, we climbed out the window," I said, shooting Viktor a dirty look. "And then this idiot got the idea to jump off the roof."

Niesha's eyebrows rose. "You jumped off the roof? Onto what?"

"We jumped from the roof of the house to the roof of the garage," Viktor said before I could say anything. "That wasn't the problem."

Remembering how I'd landed on the roof, I reached for the hem of my t-shirt and pulled it up. Niesha sucked in a breath through her teeth.

"How'd you get road rash on your stomach?"

"It's roof rash, technically," Viktor said.

"Shut up," I snapped, dropping my shirt. "That's the least of my problems." I didn't really want to move my leg again any more than I had to, so I leaned over as much as I could and pulled at the laces on my shoe. Even that bit of movement still hurt. But I managed to get it undone.

"It's swollen," Niesha said, leaning closer to peer at my ankle as I tugged on the hem of my jeans. "Is it broken?"

"Probably. I felt something crunch when I landed."

"Great." She shot a look at Viktor. He leaned back a little, as if she'd taken a physical swipe at him.

"What?"

"Do you ever think before you act?"

"I *was* thinking. I was thinking about how it would be really bad if those guys found us and we were cornered." He reached up and smoothed back a few strands of hair that had escaped his ponytail. "You think they claimed the place?"

"I wouldn't doubt it."

"King Joshua's guys?"

"Stop calling him that," I snapped, pulling my attention away from the sight of my puffy ankle and turning to glare. "And if it *was* his guys, then we're in a shitload of trouble."

"Why?"

"Because I was on a job for Joshua. I never came back. I never brought him his stuff. And now it looks like I've joined up with the boss I was supposed to rip off."

Niesha shook her head slowly. "Did you recognize those two at the house?"

"I wasn't really paying attention to who was around the last time I was in his lair."

Viktor snorted.

"Have you ever been in there?" I asked. "You'd love it. Stinks like an armpit and old cheese."

He lifted his arm and sniffed his pit. His eyes rolled back in his head, and he collapsed backward onto the grass.

"It doesn't matter if I recognized anyone," I said, turning back to Niesha. "They probably recognized me. I was in there just yesterday."

"Right." She shook her head slowly and stared off into the distance, as if in thought. Viktor was still sprawled out on the grass, perhaps taking advantage of his dramatic acting to have a little rest. I glanced at Click, only to find that he'd moved closer to my ankle and was sort of crouched over it. His hands hovered just above my skin. A soft buzz of noise came from his direction, as if he were humming to himself.

"What the hell are you doing?" I asked, but he didn't seem to notice. A moment later, he brought his hands down, gently grasping the joint. I sucked in a breath, bracing myself for the pain. But there wasn't much. He was careful not to jostle me, and the warmth of his hands felt nice. I turned back to Niesha. "So . . . what now?"

She frowned as she drew herself out of her thoughts. "Now?"

"I can't very well work for you with a broken ankle."

"It's temporary. You'll heal. Besides, you don't even know if it's broken."

"I'm pretty sure it is."

"Too bad you can't x-ray it," Viktor said lazily, not even bothering to open his eyes.

"I probably could," I said, then realized that maybe I shouldn't have let that slip. Niesha was suddenly alert.

"What do you mean?"

"Nothing."

"Léa, if you know of a doctor still in town—"

"What? I should give him up so you can raid his office for supplies?"

She looked almost hurt, and I regretted my words immediately. "No," she said slowly. "But it's always good to have resources. There are so few people with real skills here."

"Yeah, well, that's what happens when most of the adults get scared and run away."

"My aunt and uncle weren't scared," Viktor said, sitting up halfway and leaning on his elbows. "They had my cousin to think about."

"So you were in one of the group homes?"

"That place was nothing close to what you'd call a home. Which is why I didn't stay long. Nobody did. What could the guardians do? There were too many of us and not enough of them. And the ones that had volunteered to hold us in those places eventually got the heck out of here, too."

"Which is why a true adult ally would be a good thing," Niesha said. "Anyone who's stuck around this long is either a saint or an idiot. And if they're a doctor, they're probably not an idiot."

"They're not a doctor," I said.

Viktor frowned. "But you said—"

"They're not a human doctor."

"Oh." His gaze drifted over to Lex, who seemed to be enjoying the sunshine. You wouldn't have known that the little dog lying there, eyes half closed as he sniffed the gently warming air, had recently eaten part of someone's face.

"You should go," Niesha said, glancing over at Click, who still had his hands on my ankle. The heat from his grip felt almost tingly. Or maybe I had some sort of nerve damage from the break.

"Why?" I asked. "Even if it is broken, there's not much a vet will be able to do about it."

"At least you'll know. And we can work around it. Plus, if you guys are set on keeping that dog, I want to make sure he's not going to give you rabies or something."

Viktor snorted. "Doesn't look rabid to me."

"He ate someone's face," I reminded him.

"I got so hungry once, I would've eaten my own face if I could have."

"That's nasty," Niesha said. She stood up and brushed the loose grass from her hands, then looked down at us, all business. "I need to get home. I've got a couple of runners coming over later, and I should be there. You go see the vet, and then go straight home. I don't want that cache unattended for too long."

"It's secure," Viktor said.

"Sure. Just like jumping from a roof is safe."

He rolled his eyes. "I think I know how to secure a stash."

"Look, we've gone and pissed off Joshua—"

"Potentially."

"Well, I'm going to assume we have. And I don't know if that means he's going to come after me, or after my caches."

"He might not do anything."

"And he might. If he does, I don't want to be caught off guard. So just take these two to the vet and go straight home when you're done. Got it?"

"Yes, ma'am." He sat up straight and gave her a salute.

"Jesus," she said, turning away with a dismissive wave of her hand. "Just go before you *really* start to annoy me."

"It's probably too late for that," I muttered.

"Admit it!" Viktor shouted after her. "You love me!"

She just raised her middle finger and kept walking. He sucked in a gasp.

"How rude!" Turning back to me, he smiled. The ruined side of his face crinkled in all the wrong places. "So . . . I guess we have to take you to the vet."

"I guess." I pulled my leg away from Click, not really thinking. Luckily, the movement wasn't enough to cause too much pain. He quickly lifted his hands. "Thanks," I said. "That felt nice."

He smiled, though he looked a bit confused.

"Grab your dog," Viktor said to him as he grasped

my hand to help me stand up. I managed to do it on one leg, keeping the other slightly bent. "I'll carry this one, you carry that one."

"Can't you just support me so I can hop?"

"How far away is this place?"

"Main Street."

He just stared at me for a moment, blinking his mismatched eyes. And then he scooped me up into his arms once more.

"Put me down!"

"I can't support you to hop that far. I'm like a foot taller than you, so it would be super awkward."

"And this isn't?"

"What? You don't like it when a handsome guy sweeps you off your feet?"

I pretended to look around. "What handsome guy?"

He gave me a quick smile. Too quick. I looked over at Click, who had Lex nestled into his arms once more. As Viktor began to walk, keeping his mouth shut for once, I almost apologized. But that would've upped the awkwardness level even more, so I didn't say anything at all.

CHAPTER 13

A TRIP
TO THE VET

D r. Bryan's office was on the ground floor of some two-storey buildings near the centre of town. By the time we got there, the sun was high in the sky and my stomach was making its displeasure known. Loudly. And that seemed to amuse Viktor. I was kind of glad to see his real smile again, so I just let him indulge in his stupid comments as we walked down the final stretch toward the vet's office.

"Wonder if he'll have any treats," he said, pausing to hitch me up in his arms again. "Maybe if you're a good girl, he'll give you one."

"I guess that means you won't be getting anything."

"What? Why not?"

"You made me jump off a roof."

"Fair enough. But if I hadn't, we might not be going to see someone who can give you a biscuit."

"You sure it's biscuits he's giving out? Could be jerky."

"Sounds good. You going to share?"

"You going to make me jump off any more roofs?"

He peered up at the building beside us. "Not sure how we'd even get up there. I think you're safe."

"There."

"Huh? What?"

"There," I said again, pointing. The vet clinic was kind of hard to miss. The vet's name was emblazoned on the windows that ran along the front of the space, just below the waist-high frosted part that hid the floor inside from view. Maybe that was so animals in the waiting area wouldn't go nuts watching people and cars go past outside. Viktor swerved closer.

"Is this place even open?"

"The lights are on."

"Business must be awful." He paused in front of the door. "Should I put you down? Actually, maybe you should just grab the handle. Or—" He stopped talking as Click edged past us, Lex tucked awkwardly under one arm, and pried open the door. "Thanks."

The smell as we stepped inside was the same as I remembered, if a little fainter. Despite the fact that most animals had left with their humans three years earlier, the clinic looked clean and tidy and ready for patients. Although, the desk—which had once held a computer and a phone—was empty, so booking appointments would've been tricky.

"Hello?" Viktor called. I gave his shoulder a little smack, and he turned to me in surprise. "What?"

"Be quiet!"

"I thought you knew this vet."

"Yeah, but we don't know if that's who's here at the moment. And put me down."

"What if we need to make a quick getaway?"

I searched for a retort, but then a figure appeared at the door to the back hallway. I let out a sigh of relief.

"Léa?"

"Yeah. Hi, Dr. Bryan."

He didn't really look like a vet at that moment. The white coat he'd worn before the Rift, sleeves rolled up, was missing. In his plaid shirt and jeans, grey hair roughly styled, he looked like somebody's cool grandfather. Even though I was still in Viktor's arms, his attention was drawn instead to Click, and to the dog he was holding.

"Is that Lex?" he asked.

"Yeah."

He looked at me. "Where did you find him?"

"In his house." I shook my head and saw the understanding dawn in his eyes. I was glad I wouldn't have to say anything more. "Do you still have an x-ray machine?" I asked, deciding to get right to the point.

"I do. Why?"

"She thinks she broke her ankle," Viktor offered.

"Yeah, because you made me jump off a roof."

Dr. Bryan frowned. "Which ankle?"

I lifted my left leg a little, and he stepped forward to take a look. Very, very carefully, he grasped my shoe by the heel and slipped it off. It didn't hurt nearly as much as I was expecting.

"Well, it's swollen. But that can happen with a sprain, too." He waved my shoe toward the exam room. "I can do an x-ray. Not much I can do if it is broken, though. Especially if it needs surgery."

"Great," I muttered as Viktor followed him into the other room. Click trotted along behind us, holding Lex. The dog was panting again, obviously nervous. It was a good thing animals hadn't been affected by the Rift, or he probably would've been throwing Riftballs at that very moment.

Dr. Bryan dug a set of keys out of his pocket and strode to a door on the far side of the exam room that was plastered with a radiation warning. The small space beyond looked like I remembered, though it was a bit more crowded. It looked like the vet had moved some of his more valuable supplies into the locked room. I didn't blame him, especially since someone had ransacked his reception area.

"Sit up there," he said, gesturing to the x-ray table. He set aside my shoe and went to turn on the computer at the side of the windowless space. Viktor put me down on the table, and I carefully lifted my leg up onto the smooth surface. "You two, out."

"Good idea," Viktor said. "We already have superpowers. Don't need any more radiation, or we might—"

"Can you be serious for once?" I snapped. He

regarded me for a moment, his expression darkening. For whatever reason, my retorts seemed to be getting to him. "Just wait out in the waiting room. I'm not going anywhere."

He snorted. "Didn't think you were."

"Then why are you a fucking barnacle?"

Reaching up to tighten his ponytail, he turned on his heel. As he walked out of the room, he caught Click by the shoulder, forcing him to follow.

"Stuck with him, are you?" Dr. Bryan asked as he used an ancient-looking mouse to start up his x-ray app. I shrugged.

"We're all stuck with each other these days, aren't we? Small town with a big wall."

He didn't say anything to that. Not for the first time, I wondered why the vet had decided to stay in a post-apocalyptic quarantine zone. But, as always, I figured it wasn't really any of my business. People had their reasons . . . and they were often hard to hear. So I kept my mouth shut and let him do his thing. He shifted my other leg out of the way, then went and grabbed a lead apron.

"I'm surprised this machine still works," I said.

"The software's a little out of date. But it works well enough. It's a good thing I switched over to digital a few years back. If I'd still been using films, we wouldn't be doing this at all."

"It's a good thing you still have the computer."

He nodded. "I double check the lock on this room

every night. After the computer in reception got stolen, I wasn't taking any chances."

"They got your phone, too."

"Who am I going to call?"

I shrugged. "Your contacts on the outside?"

He grunted in amusement. "And they'd be able to help me . . . how?"

"What do you do when you run out of something?"

"Put in a request with the powers that be. And cross my fingers." He took a step back and reached for the machine that was suspended above the table. "Let's get these x-rays done."

We spent the next few minutes trying to get a good picture of my ankle. I felt a bit silly, rolling around on that table in a room that still smelled faintly of dog, reminding me the whole time of where I actually was. But Dr. Bryan got what he needed pretty quickly and fell into silence as he checked out the scans.

"Can we come in there yet?" Viktor called from the waiting room.

"No!" I called back. I heard the vet chuckle.

"They can if they want to. It's safe."

"That wasn't my complaint," I muttered. "Fine," I said, raising my voice. Viktor appeared in the doorway a moment later and leaned against the frame.

"Well? Can he save the leg?"

"Not funny."

"It wouldn't be a big deal. I'd just have to carry you everywhere."

"Really not funny."

He smirked, the expression twisting the scarred side of his face. Click stood behind him, absently massaging Lex's ear with one hand. The dog still didn't seem any more at ease. If he was anything like Floyd had been, he probably hated that place.

"Huh," Dr. Bryan said, turning to me. "It's not broken."

"Really?"

"Really. Not now, anyway. There's evidence of a healed fracture."

I frowned. "I sprained that ankle when I was fifteen. But the doctor told me it wasn't broken."

He shrugged. "I don't know what to tell you. Maybe they were wrong. Doctors do make mistakes sometimes. But the bone was almost certainly fractured at some point. You're lucky it healed so nicely without any casting."

"Yeah. Lucky. All I remember is the hassle of those crutches. I tripped once going up the stairs and nearly messed up the other foot."

"Good thing you didn't." He went back to the computer and started clicking the mouse again.

"If Léa's going to survive," Viktor said, "could you take a look at the dog? He looks fine to me, but *somebody* thinks he might be rabid."

Dr. Bryan's eyebrows rose as he turned around. "I highly doubt it." He stepped closer to Lex and bent down a little. "Hey, buddy. Remember me?" He slid his hand under Lex's chin and gave it a little scratch. The dog swallowed nervously. "Does he seem to be in any pain?" the vet asked.

"Not that we've noticed," I said.

"How's his appetite?"

"Uh . . ."

"He kind of ate someone's face," Viktor said, at which Dr. Bryan glanced at him sharply.

"He what?"

"His owner. Whoever that was."

The vet shook his head. "What a shame. I can't say I'm surprised, though. He didn't seem to be in particularly good health the last time I saw him."

"Um, hello," I said. "The dog ate part of a person. Isn't that a sign of . . . something?"

"In this sort of situation? It's probably a sign of extreme hunger."

"The bedroom door was closed," Viktor said. "The dog wouldn't have been able to get out."

I looked at the dog and shuddered as the horrible scene flashed through my mind again. "What if he's developed a taste for human flesh?"

Viktor snorted. "He's not a zombie dog."

"No, he's not," Dr. Bryan agreed. "Animals have a strong survival instinct. But this sort of thing usually only happens in extreme circumstances. Getting locked in a room with a dead body and slowly starving to death fits the bill." He gazed at the dog for a moment before turning back to me. "I can practically guarantee that he's not going to eat any more faces. Especially if you keep him fed."

"Easier said than done," I said, just as my stomach let out a groan of protest.

"Got any treats?" Viktor asked. "Léa could probably use one."

Dr. Bryan chuckled. "The only treats I have are medicated. Unless you have a problem with fleas, you don't want those."

"Viktor might," I said.

"Hey!" He paused, then reached up with one hand and scratched at his neck like a dog. "Well, you might be right."

"Serves you right for not bathing."

"I *bathe*. Just not enough for some people."

I turned back to Dr. Bryan. "So what do I do about my ankle?"

"Stay off it for a few weeks," he said, all business once more. "Keep it elevated for the first while. And apply some ice if you can."

"Will do," Viktor said, stepping forward to help me off the table. I pushed him away. "Are you going to be like this until you're better?"

"Maybe," I snapped. "And where the hell are we going to get ice?"

"We've got running water and a working freezer in the kitchen. I think we can figure it out."

"Oh."

"If the swelling doesn't go down," Dr. Bryan said,

"or if you start losing feeling in your toes, come back."

Viktor frowned. "Can't we call you? Our friend has a landline, so—"

"Somebody stole the clinic's only phone during the first wave of looting."

"Fair enough." He lifted me off the table. I sighed, resigned. Dr. Bryan grabbed my shoe, then handed it to me. I nestled it in my lap so I could hold on to Viktor with both hands. "Thanks for checking her out, Doc."

"You're welcome," the vet said, looking somewhat amused. "Remember, stay off that ankle for a while. And don't overdo it when you do start walking on it again. All right?"

I nodded, and Viktor carried me back to the waiting area. Dr. Bryan got the door for us and held it open so we could step out into the sunlight. As the three of us made our way up the street, heading back toward the cache house, Viktor sighed.

"What now?"

"I was hoping for a treat."

"Don't you have food at your place?"

"Yeah. But there's only so much junk food a guy can eat. I was hoping for something a little more . . . meaty."

"Dog treats?"

Lex whined and licked his chops. Viktor grunted with laughter.

"See? I'm not the only one who's disappointed."

CHAPTER 14

THE BASEMENT

The cache house looked weirdly welcoming as we walked up to it. Click, seemingly unaffected by all the walking we'd done that day, bounded up the porch steps, still carrying Lex. Viktor followed more slowly, still carrying me. For some reason, I felt really tired, even though I hadn't done much exercise at all.

"Straight to bed with you, young lady," Viktor said. I turned to him with a snort.

"It's the middle of the afternoon."

"You feel tired."

"I *feel* tired? How the hell do you know?"

"I can sense it. Just one of my many talents." He followed Click around the side of the porch. The window was already open, and the guy had just disappeared inside. "Hey, Click! Might want to get Lex to do his business. I don't want to be cleaning up any messes."

There was no response from inside the house. Viktor placed me down carefully right beside the window.

"I doubt he's got any pee in the tank," I said. "He hasn't had anything to drink all day."

"We don't know exactly when he last ate."

"Shut up." I shuddered and grasped the window frame as I hopped closer. It wasn't too hard to pull myself over the sill and stand up on one leg inside. Viktor followed, angling his long limbs through the opening, and closed the window. But I noticed he didn't lock it.

"Let's get you downstairs. Then I'll make some ice."

"I can handle stairs myself," I said as he reached for me once more.

"You're going to hop down a flight of stairs?"

"I'll go down on my butt if I have to."

He shrugged. "Suit yourself. Click's probably down there already. Make sure that dog isn't in my bed."

"Which one is your bed?"

"I'm sure you'll be able to tell by the smell."

I honestly couldn't tell if he was joking or not. He left me there and headed into the kitchen. I hopped over to the open door through which I could see a set of steps leading down. The sound of running water met my ears a moment later.

Going down on my butt was actually fairly easy, and, in no time at all, I was in the basement. It wasn't anything like Grandpa's unfinished horror with nothing but a washer and dryer, some of Grandma's homemade pickles, and a bunch of dead spiders. This was like another level of the house, completely finished and decorated. The air was a bit cooler, though.

As I stood at the bottom of the stairs, Lex trotted past me, examining every corner with a sniff. There were four doors in the hallway-like space. Two of them were open. Through the one to my left, I could see part of a great big room that seemed to be more brightly lit. The other open door was straight ahead of me, and though the lights were off in the windowless space, I could tell it was a bathroom. Lex disappeared into the shadows; a moment later, I heard a slurpy lapping sound.

"Click?" I called, hopping toward the doorway to my left. I leaned against the doorframe as I took in the sight. "Holy shit."

What might have once been a rec room looked more like a dormitory . . . for a couple of very messy guys. In addition to the two couches that had been pushed up against the far wall, there were two big beds, each of a different style. One was modern, the base made of sleek grey wood. The other was a little more ornate with a dark wooden headboard. Both were unmade but had plenty of covers and two pillows each. Click sat cross-legged on the modern one, a bag of potato chips in front of him. He appeared to be portioning out four stacks—three large ones and one much smaller.

"Your dog's drinking out of the toilet," I said. He

looked up, his golden eyes alight with what looked like happiness. He went back to the chips, plunging his hand into the bag. "Dogs don't eat potato chips. At least, they shouldn't."

"What else are we going to feed him?" Viktor asked. I startled, but managed not to let my hands flare as he edged past me into the room. "Ice is icing. Now we just have to wait." He flopped backward onto the bed with the ornate headboard, spreading his arms wide with a satisfied groan. "You should put your foot up."

"Yeah? Where do you propose I do that?"

He lifted his head to look at me. "There are two beds. Pick one."

"I'm not sleeping in your stinking bed."

"Then sleep in Click's."

"Maybe that should be up to him."

He sighed and sat up, then bent over to untie his boots. When that was done, he kicked them off and lifted his feet onto the bed.

"I can smell those things from here."

He snorted. "Yeah, right."

"I think you must've fried your olfactory nerves when you melted your face."

"Maybe. Or maybe I'm just used to it. I'm sure I'll get used to your stinky feet, too."

"I don't have stinky feet."

"No? Feet can get pretty ripe when you don't wear socks."

"I don't *have* socks."

"Why not?"

"Because one of them had to be cut off my foot. It wasn't much good after that. Didn't seem like there was any point in keeping the other one."

He was quiet for a moment, putting the pieces together. I knew he knew I was talking about the incident with my toe. But he didn't pry. Which seemed odd.

Click crunched into a chip, drawing our attention over to him. He grinned, licking the salty particles from his lips, and gestured to the piles. Viktor chuckled.

"Nice."

"If this is all you have to offer," I said, "I'm going back to Niesha's tomorrow."

"We were going to do that anyway. Her runners might have a haul."

"More snacks?"

He shrugged. "There's usually some real food, too."

"Can you cook it?"

"I," he said, placing his hand on his chest, "am an excellent cook."

"Then why did it seem like you're over at Niesha's house on a regular basis, eating her food?"

"She's the boss," he said, as if that explained it all. He stood up and swept one pile of potato chips into his hand, then nodded toward his bed. "Take a load off."

"I told you, I'm not sleeping in your stinking bed."

"You don't have to sleep. But you heard the doc. You need to put your foot up." He crunched into a chip, eyebrows raised at me. Glowering, I hopped into the room and over to his bed.

"You're not getting in this bed while I'm in it."

"Fair enough. Click and I can share."

"What about the dog?"

"He can sleep with you."

I stopped, hands braced on the mattress, and gaped at him. He laughed.

"Okay, fine. He can sleep with us. No big deal if he eats *my* face, right?" He sat heavily on the edge of Click's bed. "Where is the little nose-snacker, anyway?"

"Having a drink in the bathroom."

"That's a long drink."

Click scrambled to the other side of the bed, abandoning the chips. Viktor chuckled as he popped another snack into his mouth.

"If there's a puddle, clean it up!" He turned to me. "So, what do you want to do?"

"Do?" I asked absently as I rid myself of my shoes and crawled gingerly onto the bed. The sheets let out a whiff of stink as I moved around, but it wasn't as bad as I'd feared.

"Yeah. Unless you want to just chat until it's time to go to bed."

"Fuck, no."

He laughed. "I think I'm going to ask Niesha if she can spare any soap. Your mouth could do with a good scrub."

"I'm twenty. I can talk however I like." I bunched a

pillow against the headboard and leaned back. "When you grow up, you can use those words, too."

"Right." He snorted, then bit into another chip. "Who's going to stop me?"

"There's nobody stopping you now."

"Maybe I just don't like those words."

I shook my head. "You're weird. You know that, right?"

"Yup." He shoved the last chip into his mouth, then wiped his hands on his pants before striding from the room. I heard a door open somewhere else in the basement. A few moments later, he returned, a throw pillow in one hand.

"Where'd you get that?" I asked as he set it on the bed, then gently maneuvered my foot onto it. My first instinct was to snap at him. But he finished his caretaking quickly enough, almost as if he sensed he shouldn't linger.

"I ordered it online while I was upstairs making the ice. Talk about fast shipping."

"Do you *ever* stop?"

"Stop what?" he asked innocently.

I let out a long sigh and stared up at the ceiling as I carefully rolled my foot into the pillow. It was just soft enough to cradle my still-sore ankle like a cloud.

"This is a cache house," he said. "It's where we cache our stash."

"Pillows?"

"Why not? People love pillows." He stared at me for

a moment. I glared back. Finally, he stepped away and walked over to the small cabinet beneath the rather large TV hanging on the wall. When he crouched down and opened it up, I could see a ton of plastic boxes, as well as what looked like a video-game console, a DVD player, and a tangle of cords. "Want to watch something?"

"That thing works?"

He turned back to me with a frown. "The TV? Yeah. Well, sort of. There's no cable or streaming or anything, but our collection of DVDs is pretty good. Or we could play a game."

"I don't play video games."

"Why not?"

I shrugged. "Don't know how. Never done it."

He blinked. "You've never done it? Wow. So you've never witnessed a digital bloodbath? You're more sheltered than I thought."

Not sheltered enough, I thought, but I kept the words to myself.

"You're going to be stuck down here for a while," he said, turning back to the cabinet, "so there's plenty of time to teach you all you need to know."

I sighed. "We basically live in a fucking video game. How is it escapism if you're controlling a character with deadly magic powers?"

"I don't think we have a game like that."

"I'm just saying." Closing my eyes, I tried to get a little more comfortable. "No video games."

"Sure, Mom."

"You can play them. Just don't force me to do it."

He sighed as he rummaged through the cabinet. I felt myself sort of spinning down toward sleep, and I opened my eyes quickly, hoping to stop myself. My stomach let out an angry growl.

"Whoa. Better feed that thing," Viktor said, prying open a DVD case and lifting out the disc inside. He slipped it into the player, grabbed a remote, and headed back toward me. I shook my head quickly, and he veered over to Click's bed. "Want your chips?"

"I guess. If that's all there is."

"There's some licorice in the stash."

"Black or red?"

"Actually, I think it's purple. Some sort of weird berry flavour."

I wasn't sure what my stomach really wanted, other than to not be empty. I sighed. "I'll just have the chips."

"Don't worry," he said as he transferred the meagre pile into my outstretched hands. "We'll have something better tomorrow."

CHAPTER 15

DON'T MESS WITH THE KING

The room was still dark when I woke the next morning. The light coming in from the high window wasn't enough to really illuminate the space, and I couldn't figure out what had disturbed me. I was pretty comfortable, except for the clammy plastic bag full of melted ice that was still draped over my ankle. I stretched my arms above my head and blinked into the darkness, only to see a shadow move. I sucked in a sharp breath.

"It's just me," Viktor's voice said.

"What time is it?"

"Heck if I know."

"Then what are you doing?"

"Somebody keeps kicking me in his sleep."

"Click?"

He grunted in amusement as his shadow moved toward the foot of the bed. "Somebody with much smaller feet." There was a thump, and then a strangled sort of squeal. "Fart!"

"You better not."

"Son of a bunny." A moment later, a pink flare illuminated the room from his raised hand. He hopped a little on one foot. "You might have to share your ice with me."

"What ice? It's a bag of water."

"Good to know. So if there's a wet spot in my bed, I'll know it's not pee."

"I'm sure there've been worse things in here."

"You're probably right." He looked down at his foot, then turned his attention to the other bed. Click was still fast asleep. Lex wasn't—we'd probably woken him—but he didn't seem inclined to get up, either. Only his head was raised.

"Turn your hand off," I said, trying to get comfortable. "I might be able to get a little more sleep."

"You might. There are perks to not having a dog in the bed." He sighed and looked over at the couches . . . which didn't look very accommodating, piled high with crap the way they were. Turning to me, he raised his eyebrows.

"No."

"Come on. It's my bed! I promise I'll stay on my side."

There was a sudden shuffling noise from the other bed. Viktor raised his hand to cast more light over there, and then we could see Lex turning around in circles, tugging at the covers with his paws. He flopped down next to Click, who wrapped his arm around him, pulling him close. It looked like the boy was still asleep.

"Guess that dog's here to stay," Viktor muttered. He turned back to me. "Well?"

I sighed. It *was* his bed, after all. "Two conditions," I said at last.

"Only two?"

"One," I said as if I hadn't heard him, "you don't touch me."

"What if I do it by accident?"

"I'll give you a matching scar on the other side."

"Wow. You're a brutal one."

"I have to be."

"What's the second condition?"

I nodded my chin toward his hand. "You put that thing out. No hand farts in the bed."

"What about regular farts?"

"What do you think?"

He shrugged, but he shook his hand, extinguishing the pink glow. "Sometimes they just slip out." A moment later, I felt the bed shift. I edged sideways, as far as I could go without feeling like I was going to fall off. When the movement stopped, I heard him let out a long breath.

"What?" I asked.

"Nothing."

"Then be quiet. Let's just get some more sleep before it's time to get up."

"How's your ankle?"

"Fine. Now, shut up."

He did, leaving the room in awkward silence. I rolled my head away from him and closed my eyes.

—

When I woke again, the room was bright enough to see in, and I could smell something sort of cheesy. Artificially cheesy, but still . . . something smelled edible. My stomach growled. I looked over at the other bed. It was empty, the covers all mussed and tangled. Sitting up, I wiggled my toes and looked down at my ankle. The plastic bag of water was gone. So was something else. I frowned as I reached down and probed at the normal-looking flesh.

"Looks like my ice is magic," Viktor said. I turned to find him standing in the doorway.

"Maybe I just heal fast."

"Or maybe you were just faking it so you could get carried around."

I glared at him. "Are you serious?"

"What girl doesn't want to be swept off her feet by the handsome hero?"

"Fair enough. Seen one of those around?"

He mimed a knife to the heart, staggering against the doorframe.

"Where's Click?" I asked.

"Outside." He straightened up and strode over to

one of the couches. As he started pawing through the piles of clothes, I swung my legs off the bed and carefully set both feet on the floor. So far, so good. "You should've seen the pee Lex had. Soaked the fence." He chuckled. "Good thing he knows how to hold it. That would've wrecked Click's mattress for sure." He pulled something small and bright from the pile, then tossed it at me. I squeaked and flailed as if he'd just tossed a venomous snake in my direction. My hands flared as the pair of socks fell harmlessly to the floor.

"Don't do that!"

"What? Give you socks?" He shrugged. "Okay . . . but you kind of need them."

I shook off the pink before bending over to swipe the pair from the carpet. "I don't *need* them. It's almost summer."

"Don't you get blisters?"

"My feet are used to my shoes. Besides, doesn't Click need these more than I do?" I asked, holding them up. He just raised one eyebrow.

"You think they'd fit him?"

I regarded the socks again. They were kind of small. They might've been kids' socks, actually. The dogs and donuts all over them certainly gave me that impression. I gave one an experimental stretch.

"You don't *have* to wear them," he said. "But I've noticed you don't like showing off that toe, so . . ."

"What toe?"

"Exactly."

I dropped the socks on the bed beside me. "You don't go around hiding your face."

"Easier said than done. What would you suggest? A paper bag with a couple of eye holes?"

"Wouldn't you only need one hole?"

He frowned. "Are you always so mean in the mornings?"

"Only to people who try to force me to wear socks."

He held up his hands and shook his head. "I'm not forcing you to do anything. Wear them. Don't wear them. I was just trying to be nice."

"Well, I don't need you to be nice. In fact," I said, standing up and balancing on my right leg, "I don't need anything from you. I never asked for any of this."

"Huh."

"What's that supposed to mean?"

He tightened his ponytail and walked back to the door. "I just assumed," he said, pausing at the threshold, "that when you eat with someone, get them to carry you to the vet, and share a bed with them, it means you're a little more than passing acquaintances."

"You know what they say about assuming."

He stared at me for a moment, then turned and walked out. I heard his footsteps on the stairs a moment later.

"We're heading over to Niesha's," he called back down to me. "If you can make it up here by the time we're ready to leave, you can come. If not, you'll have to entertain yourself all day."

I wanted to retort, but the only thing in my throat seemed to be bitter regret. I rubbed my fingertips into my scalp as I closed my eyes. *What the hell is wrong with you? He's right, you know. You're being a raging bitch.*

Maybe it was hunger. Maybe it was fatigue. I didn't know.

What I *did* know was that I didn't want to be stuck in that house all day by myself. And I did like Niesha, even if she had questionable taste in lackeys. So I (very carefully) put a little weight on my left foot. I looked down, almost expecting to see somebody else's foot there. There was no pain. Maybe a little bit of discomfort. I took an experimental step forward. My ankle didn't give so much as a twang.

Sitting down on the bed, I grabbed the socks and put them on. Then I slipped on my shoes and gingerly headed for the door.

—

Viktor wouldn't stop looking at me as we walked the few blocks to Niesha's house in the damp sunlight. I tried to ignore him and just concentrate on walking. The air smelled like woodsmoke, and there was a distinct mist that hung over the neighbourhood. Click and Lex were ahead of us, the dog trotting along at Click's side and occasionally looking up at him. It was as if they'd been best friends forever.

"Are you sure you should be walking?" Viktor asked. I just shot him a dirty look.

"You're not carrying me."

"If that ankle isn't healed, you could be doing more damage."

"It isn't broken. Besides, it feels fine."

"Uh-huh."

"What's that supposed to mean?"

"Nothing," he said, but the word was loaded. He shrugged and tucked a strand of dark hair behind one ear. His ponytail looked a little worse for wear. Come to think of it, though, I hadn't seen a comb or a brush at their place.

"You still think I was faking?"

"I don't want to argue this morning."

"What makes this morning different? You're pretty fucking argumentative the rest of the time."

Even though it was the scarred side of his face that was pointed toward me, I still noticed when he clenched his jaw.

"Fine. Give me the silent treatment. It's not like you—" I broke off as he came to a sudden stop. I looked back as I kept walking. His fists were clenched, and his eyes were closed. Silent words escaped from his lips. "What are you doing?"

He didn't answer. He just kept up the clenching and mouthing. After a few seconds of that, he took a long, deep breath and opened his eyes.

"What was that all about?" I asked.

With a shake of his head, he started walking again, passing me with a few strides. "Nothing."

"It wasn't nothing," I said, jogging to catch back up to him. God, his legs were long.

"We all cope in our own ways."

"Going quiet? That's coping?"

He shrugged. "Better than being a bunny."

It took me a moment to realize what he'd just called me, in his weird way. I felt my face rush with heat. I glanced down at my hands, just to make sure they weren't flaring, too. My whole body felt hot. "Are you serious?"

"I'm not going to pry. You've obviously got some nasty spit in your past. Either that, or you're just a nasty person. But I don't think that's it."

"Prefer to see the good in people, do you?"

"Yeah. Makes it easier."

"Well, I've got news for you. Sometimes there *is* no good in people." I stormed ahead of him, following Click and the dog, who had just turned down the lane between the stone fences. Lex looked back at me for a moment, then turned and continued to trot along, his perky tail bouncing over his back. He really was kind of cute—unlike Floyd, who'd been sweet but pretty damn ugly—and I found myself thinking that it might be nice to have a dog again . . . until I remembered what Lex had done to his previous owner's face.

The smell of smoke seemed to get stronger as we walked. It wasn't unusual to smell that sort of thing;

though the town still had electricity, sometimes furnaces and heaters broke down. A decent fireplace was often the difference between a comfortable winter and a really brutal one. But the thing was, it was almost summer. The nights were cool, but not enough to justify the hassle and resources of lighting a fire. Besides, unnecessary fires were dangerous in a town without a working fire department. The second summer after the Rift, a smoky stink had settled over Kenyonville. Rumour was that a couple of blocks had burned to the ground in Rasputin's territory, the fire spreading through several banks of wood-frame townhouses before it had fizzled out. I'd never gone to check out the scene, but I had no reason to doubt the rumour. The smell had lingered for days, even in the other territories. We'd all been more careful after that, and I hadn't heard (or smelled) any other signs of a major fire since.

Well, until that morning.

A sick feeling began to spread through me, even though I wasn't sure exactly why. Niesha's house had electric heat, so there wouldn't have been any reason for her to start reckless fires. I glanced at Click, who was frowning. He came to a sudden stop at the same moment that Viktor's footsteps behind me broke into a run.

"No. Dang it, no!"

Click was just standing in front of the open gate, staring. Lex—seemingly unaware of the weird vibe that had fallen over the humans, sniffed along the edge of the fence. Viktor pushed past Click and stumbled into Niesha's yard. As I walked a little closer, the view shifted, and I could see past the trees to the house.

Or what was left of it.

"Niesha!" Viktor shouted as he ran toward the charred ruin. "Niesha!" His voice cracked. He stopped at the base of the porch steps, which were blackened but still standing, and bent over, hands on knees. Smoke rose from the ruins, and I could see a few fingers of flame deep within the rubble. "Dang it, Niesha!" he screamed.

I stopped in the open gate and stared. The wrongness of the sight was compounded by Viktor's sobs as he bowed his head, turning away from the house. He began to cough, and the sound was almost hysterical.

"Viktor."

He straightened up, startling me with his suddenness, and turned toward the source of the voice. Huddled against the back fence in her pyjamas, couched in the long grass that had yet to be mowed, sat Niesha. Long wisps of loose curls floated out around her head. Her dark skin was smudged with soot, and an even darker look dwelled within her nearly black eyes. Viktor took a hesitant step toward her, almost as if he wasn't sure she was real. When he realized she wasn't a ghost, he barrelled toward her, skidding on his knees in the wet grass as he threw his arms around her body.

"What the hell happened?" I asked when it seemed that someone had to take control of the conversation. Click edged past me into the yard, Lex following. The dog immediately went to investigate the trunk of the ornamental tree on the far side of the space.

Niesha's gaze was fixed on what was left of her house. I wasn't sure if she'd even heard me. I took a step toward her, but then she opened her mouth.

"What do you think?"

"Yeah, but how?"

She blinked slowly. Viktor released his grip and drew away, but he kept a gentle hand on her shoulder.

"Joshua?" he asked.

"Who else?"

"But why?" I asked. They both turned to look at me.

"Do you really need to ask a question like that, Léa?" Niesha said, her voice gravelly. She coughed and shook her head. "Enough."

"Yeah, enough is enough," Viktor said. "I'm tired of that donkeybutt and his—"

"No." She shook her head as she grabbed the phone that was sitting beside her in the long grass. "I'm done." She stood up, looking decades older than she actually was. "He won."

"Like heck he did! You've still got the cache houses. And you can live with us. There's plenty of room."

She turned to him and fixed him with a look I couldn't really decipher. Nonetheless, a shiver ran down my spine. He must've had a similar reaction, because he stood up quickly, shaking his head.

"Whatever you're thinking of doing, it's not worth it."

"Oh, it'll be worth it."

"Niesh, you're not that kind of—"

She held up her hand to cut him off. "You have no idea, Viktor. You're just a child."

"Excuse me?"

"I know you mean well, but you don't get it."

He folded his arms in a posture that looked distinctly pouty. "Great. Another woman's going to give me a hard time."

"I'm not giving you a hard time. I'm just stating the facts. You don't understand." She waved her phone at the ruins of the house. "I promised my parents I'd take care of it."

"You think they'd expect you to put out a fire all by yourself?"

"No, I think they expected me to not go making enemies that would burn down their house." She glanced at me, then shook her head. I clenched my hands into tight fists as I felt a hot anger build up within me.

"Fine," I said, my voice low. "Blame me."

"She's not," Viktor said.

"Yeah, she is. And she's right. If you hadn't met me, none of this would've happened. She'd still have her house."

"You'd still be alone."

"So what?" I said, my voice dangerously close to a shout. "So fucking what? It's not up to you to take in every stray you come across."

"You're not a—" he began, then stopped short as he saw Niesha begin to pick her way toward the gate, the sneakers that she'd somehow managed to slip on shuffling through the overgrown grass. "Where are you going?"

"Where do you think?"

He jogged after her, then planted himself in her path. She glared up at him.

"Move your ass."

"I'm not going to let you do something you'll regret."

"You're not going to *let* me?" She let out a humourless laugh. "And you think you have any say in what I do?" Shoving him aside, she stormed to the gate. "You can do what you like, Viktor. But I'm doing this. And I will *not* regret it."

CHAPTER 16

THE 36-MONTH PLAN

I didn't know what to do. Despite the fact that it had only been a couple of days since I'd been on my own, I was kind of used to having company now (annoying as it was sometimes), and I didn't relish having to fend for myself again. Besides, what would I have done? I'd already burned bridges with Joshua, and he'd burned down Niesha's house. I wasn't exactly on the best terms with C-Roy anymore, and Permanent Marc was *not* an option. There were a couple of other bosses in town, but I didn't know them—I only knew *of* them, and based on what I'd heard, I wasn't sure if I would be willing to pledge allegiance to either of them. There were worse things than being alone and hungry.

Being with Niesha, Viktor, and Click wasn't one of those things. So, after a few long moments spent staring at the smoking remains of Niesha's once-welcoming house, I followed them.

The walk to Joshua's lair seemed to take a lot longer than it should have. Maybe it was because nobody—not even chatty Viktor—was saying anything. Maybe it was simply because I had no idea what was going to happen when Niesha confronted the little pissant about her house. Well, I had an idea, but it wasn't a pleasant one. We were dealing with a pissed-off boss with an axe to grind, another boss with an ego the size of a stadium, and pinkhands thrown into the mix. On top of everything else, Joshua's goons had guns. Who knew if they were loaded? I didn't want to find out the hard way.

By the time we made it to the strip mall that housed Joshua's throne room, the sun was high overhead. Even on that side of town, you could still smell a bit of smoke. When I looked back the way we'd come, though, all I could see was a sort of white mist, like a low-hanging cloud.

"Might want to stay out here with that thing," Viktor said to Click as we approached the building. Lex had been trotting along obediently the whole way. As we came to a stop, he looked up at his best friend, waiting for a command. But Click just bent down and scooped him up.

"There's safety in numbers," Niesha said absently as she slipped her phone into the pocket of her pyjama pants.

"I thought you said that dog was a potential ransom situation."

"I don't think Joshua will be interested."

"What if he is?"

"Then we hand the dog over." She strode toward the cell phone store without another word, leaving Viktor to gape after her.

"Are you farting serious?" he asked, but she didn't respond. He turned to Click. "Stay out here."

Click frowned at him.

"If Joshua wants that dog, Niesha's just going to hand him over. You think I'm going to be able to stop her?"

Stepping forward, Click reached out and grabbed Viktor's wrist, only to pull his hand onto Lex's scruffy head. Viktor let out a long sigh.

"Yeah, he's growing on me. But—"

"Bah-dee," Click said, following up the utterance with a click at the back of his throat.

"What?"

Click repeated the word. Viktor's confused frown deepened.

"Oh," I said as it dawned on me. "Buddy." Click turned to me, his golden eyes alight. "That's his name?"

"Thought his name was Lex," Viktor muttered, drawing his hand away.

"Dr. Bryan called him 'buddy,' remember?"

"So?"

"So, obviously, Click thought that was his name. Besides, Buddy is a perfectly good name for a dog."

"Bah-dee," Click corrected me, emphasizing the click at the end. I tried to imitate the sound, which only made him smile.

"Well, whatever his name is now," Viktor said, "if you want to keep him safe . . ."

But all that happened was that Click's arms tightened around the dog, cradling him in an embrace that seemed to say: "Nothing is going to hurt my best friend." I sighed and looked away, searching for Niesha, who was waiting—rather impatiently—closer to the door.

"Come on," I said as I began to walk, hoping the guys would follow.

Niesha frowned at the sight of the dog in Click's arms, but she didn't say anything about it. She tried to smooth her wayward curls, giving up a moment later as they sprang stubbornly back out. "You let me do the talking," she said, staring directly at Viktor. He widened his eyes.

"Why are you looking at me?"

"Because you have a big mouth."

"So I'm not allowed to tell that donkeybutt how I feel about him burning down my friend's house?"

"First of all, I'm not your friend. I'm a boss. We don't have friends."

He raised an eyebrow. "Since when?"

"Since I had my fucking house burned down. Jesus Christ, Viktor. Do I really have to explain this to you? This town . . . It's not reality. Not like we were used to.

We can't have friends. We can't form attachments." Her gaze drifted to the dog.

"Like heck we can't."

She looked back up at him, a dull expression in her eyes. "Easy for you to say."

"I already told you: You can live with us. No problem."

"And what if that's not what I want? What if I don't want to live like this for the next sixty years, or however long it's going to be?"

"You don't have much of a choice. It is what it— Wait!" he cried as she turned and stormed toward the door. The three of us hurried after her, and Viktor managed to catch the door on the backswing after she stormed into the shadowy depths of the former store.

The fluorescent light over Joshua's throne flickered and buzzed, as if annoyed by the person who lounged under it. He was just as I'd left him, installed in his stupid recliner, head tilted back so he could look down his nose at us. I suspected he'd known we were coming, because I kind of doubted he spent all day with his ass planted there. (Then again, maybe he was just that lazy.)

"You could've knocked," he said, flipping the lever on the side of the recliner so he could sit up straight. Niesha planted herself right in front of him and fixed him with a sharp glare. Viktor immediately positioned himself at her side like some sort of overzealous bodyguard. Click joined them a moment later, leaving me cowering by the door like a nervous idiot.

"So could you," Niesha said, but Joshua's attention slid over to me, and he didn't seem to hear her.

"You've got a lot of nerve coming back here."

I shrugged, though my heart was pounding in my throat. I kept my hands tightly clenched into fists and behind my back, lest they erupt in pink where he could see them.

"I guess you don't have my stuff."

"The stuff you asked her to steal from my cache," Niesha said, drawing his attention back to her.

He held up his hands. "It's just business."

"And last night? That was business, too?"

"You were in my house. I had to send a message."

Niesha narrowed her eyes. "That dump on Havilland and Monroe? Since when was that *your* house?"

"Since I claimed it." He leaned forward. "Do you make a habit of breaking into other people's homes?"

"Do you?"

He leaned back in his throne and tented his fingers. "If there's no living owner, yeah."

"So you knew about—"

"My guys hadn't got around to chucking the stinker yet."

Niesha grunted. "Grow up and show a little respect."

Joshua's eyebrows drew together, darkening his expression. "That house was off limits. I claimed it. Didn't you notice the ticket?"

"The door was open when I found the place," I said, causing everyone to turn to me. I shuffled back a step, feeling the weight of all those gazes. "I called out. Nobody was there."

"Oh, someone was there," Joshua said. He let out a snort of laughter. "You think my guys were going to answer?"

My heart sank. Of course there could've been people in the house that day. They'd simply left the door open while they were checking the place out.

"I've been watching that house for a while," Joshua went on. "When that dog stopped barking, I knew the old bugger had probably died."

"So you thought you'd just take his house?" Niesha asked. She shook her head. "What's wrong with the places you've already got?"

"Most of them are too far from the action." He shrugged. "I'd like to be able to keep an eye on the competition."

"So you want a house right on the doorstep of someone else's turf?"

"Why not?"

"What's your problem?" Viktor asked, the words bursting out of him like he couldn't contain them for another second. Niesha shot him a furious look, but he ignored her. "Your goons chased us away. You didn't need to 'send a message.'"

Joshua smirked and turned to Niesha. "You let your lapdog speak?"

"Can't seem to shut him up. But he's got a point."

"There's a code. There has to be. You trespassed in my new house. You had to face the consequences." He held up his hands helplessly. "Fair's fair."

"Accidentally trespassing hardly warrants burning down my house, you fucking asshole!"

Joshua jerked as if Niesha had physically slapped him. The colour drained from his face, leaving him looking more pasty than ever. "I didn't burn down your house."

"No? Want to see the smoking pile of rubble?"

He sat forward and ran his fingers through his greasy hair. "Shit."

"Don't play innocent, you little—"

"I didn't know," he said. "Seriously. I sent a couple of runners over last night with some cans of spray paint." He held up his hands. "That's all. I swear."

"Sure."

"Why would I want to burn down your stupid house? You think I want more enemies?"

"I don't know what the fuck you want," she spat. "But I'm going to tell you what I want. And you're going to give it to me, because you fucking *owe* me. Understand?"

Joshua looked like he was trying to process the most complicated math problem in the world. Niesha was kind of hard to figure out sometimes—especially at that moment when she was full of fury—and the little pissant didn't seem to know how to respond. Or *if* he should respond. He just sat there, a stupid look on his pimply face, and stared at her glowering expression.

"Understand?" she prompted when it seemed like he might never answer at all. But the question seemed to snap him out of whatever quasi-compassionate state he might've momentarily been in, and the smarmy expression slid back onto his face.

"Do you understand how this all works? I don't give away anything for free. If you want something—"

"You . . . owe . . . me." Her voice was dark and slow.

"I don't owe you for a mistake made by some fuck-faced kid."

"He's *your* fuck-faced kid."

"He made his own choices. If you're pissed, take it up with him. Not me."

Niesha looked like she was about to spit vipers at the guy. Even Viktor seemed awed enough that he knew better than to open his mouth again.

"But now I'm curious," Joshua said, tilting his head and pretending to look interested. "What is it that you want? What is it that I have that you don't?"

"A headquarters that smells like feet," Viktor muttered. Niesha's hand whipped out sideways to smack him in the stomach.

"A phone," she said.

Joshua snorted. "A phone? And what are you going to do with that? You know they don't work anymore. I guess you could take pictures with it . . ."

"Your landline, asshole."

"Who says I have a landline?"

"This store has one of the remaining working landlines in town. It's common knowledge." She folded her arms across her chest. "Well?"

"I'm not giving you my phone."

"I'm not asking for the *phone.* I just want to make a call."

"To who?"

"None of your business."

He held up one finger in a scolding sort of gesture. "Ah, but it's my phone. That makes it my business."

She glared at him, eyes narrowing slowly. "Fine," she said at last, almost spitting the word. "My parents."

"Why would you want to call them?"

"I thought maybe I should tell them about their house. You know, since you burned it down." She took a tiny step forward. The shuffling movement was enough to make Joshua flinch, even though she wasn't really doing anything threatening like whipping out pinkhands. "Like I said . . . you owe me."

"Nope. All's fair in the Rift Zone. Stuff happens." He stroked the few pathetic hairs on his chin like a corny villain. "But I guess it wouldn't hurt to let you make one call. You got their number?"

She didn't dignify his stupid question with a response. He shrugged and waved his hand toward the counter at the back of the space.

"Can I have a little privacy?" she asked.

He snorted. "Where do you expect me to go? No, I'm staying right here. Anything you have to say can be said in front of me."

"Asshole."

"Do you want to use my phone or not?"

"Is being nice to you part of the deal?"

He shook his head and waved his hand to point over at the counter again. She edged past Viktor and started to walk over there. "Wait."

She stopped and turned back to him, rolling her eyes. "What?"

"You haven't paid me yet."

"Are you serious? Does it look like we have anything to pay you with?" She held her arms out to the sides as if to demonstrate her relative poverty. "You did just burn down my house."

"Now, we all know you wouldn't have kept your entire stash in one place. The address I sent Léa to the other day has plenty of stuff."

"Yeah?"

"Yeah."

"And how do you know that?"

"I have my sources." His gaze slid over to me.

"Don't make me look like some sort of double agent," I snapped.

"Aren't you?"

"How could I be? I don't work for you."

"You did."

"Maybe I got a better offer."

"Oh . . . I get it. You fucking White-Eye McMeltyface over there?"

"Yeah. All day and all night. For two days straight. Why do you think I never came back?"

Viktor shook his head. I couldn't tell if he was amused or not; the twitching around his mouth might've been suppressed laughter or rage.

"Will everybody just shut up?" Niesha said. "Fine. You want weed? Snacks? Make a list."

Joshua shook his head. "That stuff's easy enough to get."

"So what do you want?"

His gaze drifted to the dog and stuck there. Click noticed, too, and his arms tightened.

"No," Viktor said.

"Why not? I've always wanted a dog."

"You don't want that one. He ate part of someone's face."

"Is that what happened to you?"

Niesha turned to Click. "Give him the dog."

Click's golden eyes grew huge. He opened his mouth, and I almost expected him to say something. But he didn't. He just took a step back, holding Buddy tight.

"Click, give him to me." She reached out and grabbed the dog, who startled. I was almost afraid Niesha was going to end up with a chunk out of *her* face, but instead of a growl, all we heard was a whine. She marched over to the throne and plunked the dog on Joshua's lap. "There. You have a dog. Congrats. Can I use your phone now?"

"Are you serious?" Viktor asked, staring at Niesha in disbelief. "That's not your call to make."

"If you're going to give me a hard time," she said, fixing him with a hot glare, "you can leave. I never asked you to come in the first place."

"Excuse me for wanting to help my friend."

"We're not friends," she said, storming over to the counter. Joshua let her go. He still looked a little stunned himself. The dog was just standing there on his lap, trying not to let his paws slip. He looked over at Click and let out a heartbreaking whine.

"Bah-dee," Click said, his golden eyes bright with tears. Joshua took one look at him and started to laugh.

"Seriously?" He gingerly put his hands around the dog so he could lean forward a bit. "What's the matter, retard? Got attached, did you?"

Viktor's hand snapped up like a shot, fingers flaring pink. Joshua whipped his head toward him.

"Put that away."

"What did you just call my friend?"

"How can you be friends with a retard?"

Viktor's mouth twitched. His fingers twitched. But the pink energy stayed where it was, swirling around his hand. On the far side of the room, Niesha began to speak, keeping her voice low. When she saw me staring at her, she ducked down behind the counter. What little I had been able to make out became a mumbled murmur.

With a grunt of distress, Click spun around and barrelled toward me. I backed up, my heart in my throat, and watched as he pushed open the door and hurtled through it. The sound of his sandals slapping on the pavement as he ran across the abandoned parking lot echoed in my ears until the door swung closed once more.

"It's just a *dog*," Joshua said, awkwardly patting Buddy's head. The dog flinched.

"Not to Click." Viktor flicked his fingers, sending up a few sparks of pink. "You better take good care of him."

"Or what?" He tilted his head back in that haughty way he had and stared down his greasy nose. "There's a code, Crinkleface McGee. You really want to test me?"

"Nobody's testing anyone," Niesha said, stepping out from behind the counter and striding over to Viktor. "Let's go."

"But—"

"Thanks for the phone call."

"No problem," Joshua said. "It was worth it."

Viktor watched as Niesha walked over to the door, his expression a mask of disbelief. "That's it? You're just going to give away Click's best friend?"

"You're his best friend, Viktor. It's better this way. Trust me."

"Like heck, it's better."

"She's right," Joshua said as Niesha pushed open the door and stepped outside. "I got the thing I wanted. You got the thing you wanted."

"I didn't want any *thing*," Niesha said. She stormed off, letting the door swing shut behind her.

Joshua shrugged. "Then I got the thing I wanted."

Viktor took a threatening step forward. "You better take care of that dog."

"Of course I will. We'll fix him up nice. Won't we?"

"Fix him . . . up?" Viktor said slowly with a glance at me. My eyes widened. I didn't like that choice of words any more than he did.

"Yeah. A little salt and pepper . . . I might even have a bit of leftover garlic powder."

"Farting heck," Viktor said. "What's the matter with you? You don't joke about that."

"I'm not joking," Joshua said matter-of-factly as he grabbed Buddy around the middle like a ham and lifted him toward the goon on his right. "Meat is hard to find these days."

CHAPTER 17

A GREAT ESCAPE

My vision flashed red with hot panic as my hands flared. Viktor looked at me in desperation, his hand still wavering in the air. He was too close to take any sort of warning shot; Joshua would most likely be hit, and that was the very last thing we needed. But if we didn't do something . . .

"Lex!" I screamed, pushing out the word with as much force as I could. It had the desired effect. The dog, hearing his original name, startled and flailed, breaking Joshua's tenuous grasp. He fell to the floor, stumbled, and skittered away from the throne. I raised my hands. Viktor might've been too close, but I wasn't. I hurled the two Riftballs toward the back of the throne. Joshua ducked as the sizzling splashes rained down over his head.

There was so much swearing in the next few seconds that I wasn't sure who was saying what. Even

Viktor might've let something slip as he raced over and scooped up Buddy, who was cowering on the floor. Then he bolted for the door. I pushed it open and held it, watching as Joshua stood up and threw his hands out to the sides, drawing on the Rift energy with his pure rage.

"What the *fuck?*" he spat, staring directly at me, the only one stupid enough to still be in that ridiculous throne room/cell phone store. "You little whore."

"You throw those Riftballs, and the gloves are off. The code is finished."

"You can't just break the fucking code."

"You're the one who sent me to a ticketed house, asshole. How does that fit in with the code?"

"I wasn't the one breaking in, was I?"

"No. You get other people to do your dirty work like a coward."

His eyes bugged. "What did you just call me?"

"Coward. A pissy little boy who breaks the code by burning down a rival boss' house."

"I didn't order that. It was an accident."

"Yeah. Sure." My whole body shook as I stood there, staring at his stupid pinkhands. I took a deep breath and raised my gaze to meet his. "We're *not* even. You mess with Niesha, you mess with me. So if you try anything else, who knows what might *accidentally* burn down. Got it?"

"Bitch."

"Got it, asshole?"

"Get out of my store!"

Gladly, I thought, edging through the door I was still holding open. I didn't turn my back on him until I was outside and so far into the sunlight that I could no longer see inside his dim little lair. Then I turned and ran.

Niesha and Viktor were waiting on the far edge of the parking lot, sitting on an overturned newspaper box. By the time I reached them, I had a stitch in my side. I skidded to a stop in front of them, breathing hard.

"Where's Click?" I wheezed.

Viktor shook his head and looked down at the dog who was snuggled into his lap, looking rather traumatized. I turned to Niesha.

"What the hell was that?" I asked, spitting the words. "You were going to give away Click's dog! You know what Joshua was planning for him, right?"

She shook her head and gave Viktor a sideways glance. "I wasn't going to give his dog away, Léa."

"But you—"

"What kind of person do you think I am?"

"I honestly have no idea," I said. The tingle in my hands made me look down, and I realized my fingers were still flaring pink. I shook them out quickly before I felt tempted to use them on Niesha. "So you lost your house. Big deal. You think nobody else has lost their home? You think we haven't lost way more than that?"

"I didn't say—"

"You gave up," I growled, "and you handed over Click's dog to that fucker. He was going to *eat* him."

"I know."

"So why—"

She held up her hand. "I wasn't going to let it get that far. We might all live by one overarching code. But that doesn't mean we don't have our own smaller ones."

I turned to Viktor in confusion. He paused in stroking Buddy's ears to look up at me with a sad smile.

"What did you do?" I whispered.

"What we always planned on if we ended up in a situation like that," Niesha said. "We don't leave anyone behind. Well, *I* don't. I can't speak for this guy." She nudged Viktor with her elbow.

"Did Click know?" I asked.

Viktor shook his head. "He's already the sweetest guy you'll ever meet. We weren't sure if he could've gone along with a deception like that. So we had to make it seem real."

"Well, we better find him," I said, "because right now he thinks that you two handed his dog over to Joshua to be dinner."

Niesha stood up and brushed her hands together. "We were just waiting for you." She watched as Viktor unfolded his long legs and stood. "Let's find Click. And then we all need to talk."

—

Click hadn't gone far. We found him a block away, hunched miserably in a wayward shopping cart that someone had wedged between a couple of parked cars. Tears poured down his cheeks as he sat there, eyes closed, quietly crying. I shot Viktor a dirty look. He at least had the decency to look guilty.

"Click?" He stopped in front of the cart. But Click didn't open his eyes or look up. He dragged the sleeve of his denim jacket under his nose. With a sigh, Viktor carefully placed the dog into his best friend's lap. The boy jerked and finally opened his eyes, only to find Buddy staring up at him. The tail began to wag. And then the kissing started.

"Bah-dee!"

"Careful," Viktor said as he watched the dog's pink tongue make quick work of the salty tears. "He might get a taste for human flesh again." Niesha whacked him on the arm. "Ow! What?"

"Let's go home," she said.

"You have no home."

"Your home, then."

"I thought you didn't want to live with us."

She shook her head. "It'll only be temporary."

"Good. Because we already have one girl living with us, and it's totally cramping my style."

I snorted. "Because you can't jerk off whenever you want?"

"Partly."

Niesha laughed softly. But then the light died from

her eyes. She watched the reunion in front of her, an inscrutable expression on her face.

"You okay?" Viktor asked.

"Just thinking."

"Looks difficult."

"Must be. You avoid it whenever you can." She waved her hand at Click. "Out you get. We need to get going. Joshua's probably pissed."

"Let him be," Viktor said.

"You want him to burn something else down? I want to get back to the cache house before he decides to do something stupid."

"I don't think he will," I said. She and Viktor both turned to me.

"Why?" Viktor asked. "What'd you do? Lob some pinkballs at his face?" His expression brightened. "Did you make me a twin?"

"No. One of you is enough."

"Dang."

"I just pointed out that there's a code. If anything happens now . . ."

"We'll know exactly who to blame," Niesha said thoughtfully. "Right. He's probably not going to try anything. Not immediately, anyway."

Click held Buddy under one arm and clambered out of the shopping cart. After a quick squeeze, he placed the dog on the ground. Buddy just stared up at him as if waiting for a command.

"What did you want to talk about?" I asked as we

set off in the direction of the cache house. "Can't we talk about it here?"

"Is it something big?" Viktor asked. "If it is, I think I need to eat first."

Niesha snorted. "You got food?"

"Sort of."

"We'll hit the cache on Maple later. I think there should still be some packets of mac and cheese."

He pretended to gag. "That military-issue stuff that tastes like feet?"

"It's either that or whatever you've got in your cache."

"I'd rather have a beer."

"That's not legal," she said. "Besides, that's not food. And you wonder why teenage boys make lousy bosses."

"Hey! I'm offended."

"Why? You're not a boss. And you're most definitely a teenage boy. Are you offended by the truth?"

He sniffed dramatically and turned away, mouth twitching. Niesha turned to me.

"You agree, right?"

I held up my hands. "I'm not getting involved."

"Too late," Viktor said, clapping his hand on my shoulder. "You're involved. And you're stuck with us, whether you like it or not."

"Great."

Niesha shook her head. "It kind of is. It'll be nice to have a bit of feminine energy to balance out . . .

whatever that is," she said, waving her hand at Viktor and Click.

"It's still three against two," Viktor said. He pointed at the dog who was trotting along at Click's side, seemingly recovered from his little ordeal of almost ending up as dinner. He veered off to sniff at a tuft of greenery, only to run back to Click when he'd satisfied his curiosity.

"The dog doesn't count."

"Sure he does!"

"Only if the three of you are going to sit around together and lick your balls," I muttered.

Viktor burst out laughing. Niesha shook her head and turned to me.

"*Thank* you," she said. She didn't have to say what for.

———

The encounter with Joshua must've taken more out of us than we thought, because when we got back to the cache house (which was, thankfully, untouched), we all fell asleep before we could do much else. Including eat. When I woke up to find the afternoon sun streaming down into the high basement windows, my stomach let out such a growl that I clamped my hands over it in embarrassment.

"Good afternoon to you, too," Niesha said. She was sitting cross-legged at the bottom of Viktor's bed (which was now apparently the girls' bed), plucking at a small bag of Cheeznudles. She held it out to me, and I lunged for it, snagging a few of the orange-dusted snacks before I realized how wild I must've looked. "Don't worry. I'm going to send them out in a few minutes to get something a little more nourishing."

"Where are they?" I asked, because I'd noticed the emptiness of the other bed.

"Took the dog outside to pee. But they must've gotten distracted by a shiny object or something."

I crunched on the salty snack and glanced nervously at the window. Niesha upended the bag and tipped the last of the Cheeznudle dust into her mouth.

"This is so nasty," she muttered.

"At least they're edible."

"Barely. And I wasn't talking about the snack so much as . . ." She waved her hand, indicating the room, just as I heard thumping on the stairs. Before either of the guys came into view, Buddy bounced into the room, tail bobbing jauntily. He paused and looked back to make sure his friends were coming.

"What was that?" Viktor asked. He took a flying leap onto his bed, twisting in midair to land on his back. "You dissing our pad?"

Niesha smirked. "Kind of hard not to. What's that smell?"

"I don't smell anything. It's probably you."

"Bah-dee," Click said, at which Niesha laughed.

"No, it's not the dog. I'm pretty sure it's a couple of sweaty guys."

"And Léa," Viktor added. I glared at him until he grinned. "So," he said, turning back to Niesha, "we're all here, and we're all awake. What did you want to talk about?"

She nodded and set the empty Cheeznudle bag aside. Click, sensing that something important was about to happen, went and sat on the edge of his bed. Buddy jumped up beside him a moment later, then proceeded to roll his body in between the pillows. "We can't keep doing this," Niesha began.

"Doing what?" Viktor asked. "Surviving?"

"Is that really what we're doing?"

He shrugged awkwardly. "So far."

"It's not enough. Not anymore."

"What's the plan? Find an abandoned mansion and live the high life?" He pushed himself up on his elbows. "Ooh! Can you find one with a pool?"

She made a face. "Do you honestly think a pool is going to be in swimmable condition after three years? In any case, no. That's not what I meant."

"Then what—"

"If you'd just shut up for a sec, maybe I could tell you."

He widened his eyes and turned to Click. "She's got a *brilliant plan*," he said, pitching his voice toward the dramatic. "So special. So secret."

"So close to regretting my decision to tell you," she muttered. "But I kind of have to."

"Why?"

"Because I'll need your help."

"With what?" he asked, sounding suspicious. "Are we going to repopulate the world? Do you need me to be the Adam to your Eve?"

"Jesus Christ," she said, though she almost looked like she was trying not to smile. "Do you want me to go to jail?"

"Why would you go to jail? You're not *that* much older than me."

"True. But if you come anywhere near me with the intent to repopulate, I might end up charged with attempted murder."

"I can't tell if you're joking or not."

"Doesn't matter. It's not happening. Besides, we don't need to repopulate anything. The rest of the world is fine, going merrily about their lives while everyone in Kenyonville is living in hell."

"Well . . . it's more like limbo, really. It's not *that* bad."

"Some boss wanted to eat your friend's dog."

"Okay, fine." He shook his head slowly, studying her face. "But what are you going to do about it?"

She didn't say anything, and the pause seemed to swallow up the room. Viktor and I exchanged a look, then turned back to her as she took a deep breath.

"I," she said, "am getting the hell out of this night-mare. And you guys are coming with me."

ALSO BY
NISSA HARLOW

Two Between Worlds
The Last Minute
No Such Thing
Elements of Mind: The Complete Quartet

<u>Generation Rift</u>
Nothing Close to Home
Escape From the Zone
So Lost Are the Foes
All the Scars of Hope

ABOUT THE AUTHOR

Nissa Harlow wanted to be a writer from the time she was a small child, but it took a while before she finally did anything about it. In the meantime, she worked as a volunteer day-camp counsellor, a movie extra, and a digital-photo editor. She even once worked on a conveyor belt in a chocolate factory (which was as stressful—and delicious—as it sounds).

These days, she lives in British Columbia, Canada and writes stories about friendship, love, and healing, all embellished with a touch of the fantastic.